The Eridanos Library 1

Robert Musil

Posthumous Papers
of a Living Author

Translated by Peter Wortsman

Eridanos Press

FIC

Contents

Ill-Tempered Observations

Unstorylike Stories

The Blackbird

Foreword

Why posthumous papers? Why of a living author?

There are poetic estates that also happen to be great gifts; but as a rule, literary legacies bear a suspicious resemblance to everything-must-go store clearance sales and cheap bargains. The popularity that such work nonetheless enjoys may indeed derive from the fact that the reading public has a forgivable weakness for a poet who for the last time lays claim to their attention. However the case may be, and whatever questions may arise as to whether such a legacy may be truly worthwhile or merely of some worth, might lead one to suppose—I at any rate have decided to forestall publication of my own last literary effects before the time comes when I will no longer have a say in the matter. And the most dependable way to make sure of this is to publish it myself while still alive, whether this makes sense to everyone or not.

But can a poet* still speak of being alive? Has not the poet of the German nation long since outlived himself? It certain-

*The English language offers no adequate equivalent to the German *Dichter*, a term that encompasses poetic as well as prose stylists whose work constitutes high art. The word *Poet* is as close as we can get. This, in any case, is the decision we have followed throughout the book. (*Translator's note.*)

ly looks that way, and strictly speaking, as far back as I can think, it has always looked that way; the situation has recently only entered a decisive chapter. The age that brought out the pre-fab custom-made shoe, and the tailor-made suit to fit all sizes, also appears to want to bring out the pre-fab poet, who is put together out of ready-made inner and outer parts. Almost everywhere these days, the made-to-measure poet lives completely cut off from life, but even so does not share with the dead the ability to do without roof, food, and drink. Life is so kind to a posthumous request! This fact has had some bearing on the title I chose for this little book and on its creation.

One ought naturally to go about selecting one's last words with that much more care, even if their finality is only a sham. To publish nothing but little tales and observations amidst a thundering, groaning world; to speak of incidentals when there are so many vital issues; to vent one's anger at phenomena that lie far off the beaten track: this may doubtless appear as weakness to some, and I will readily admit that I had all kinds of doubts regarding the decision to publish. But then a certain difference in size has always existed—and this had somehow to be taken into consideration—between the weight of poetic utterances and the six thousand, two-hundred million cubic foot mass of earth that zooms through space untouched by poetry. Second, I trust that I may be permitted to refer back to my major opus,* which may suffer less from the lack of cohesive structure perhaps so evident here. Continued work on that book meanwhile demanded that I publish this book. And finally: When this book was suggested to me, and the little parts out of which it was to be constructed lay once again before me, I recognized, or so I thought, that they were after all more durable than I had feared.

Almost all of these little pieces were written and published between 1920 and 1929; but a number of them, those called "Pictures" in the Table of Contents, derive from earlier

*Der Mann ohne Eigenschaften (The Man without Qualities).

efforts. Such is the case with "Flypaper," which appeared in a magazine as far back as 1913 under the title of "Roman Summer"; and "Monkey Island" also dates back to that time, which I mention here because one could otherwise take them for fabricated revisions based on later circumstances. In fact, they were actually a look ahead, directed toward flypaper and a cohabitation of apes; but such prophecies are likely to occur to every man who observes human life in the tiny traits by which it carelessly reveals itself, to every man who pays attention to the "loitering" sensibilities, which, apparently, up until a certain hour that stirs them up, "have nothing to say," and harmlessly express themselves in our actions and our choice of surroundings.

Something similar, though largely in the opposite sense, might likewise be alleged in defense of "Ill-tempered Observations" and "Unstorylike Stories." They visibly wear the historical moment of their inception, and the mockery in them refers back in part to bygone days. Their form also reveals their background, for they were written for news-papers, with their inattentive, motley, inordinately large readerships. No doubt they would have turned out otherwise had I written them, as I did my books, with just myself and my friends in mind. Here, in particular, was the question that had to be answered: Is it permissible to republish this sort of thing? Any revision would have necessitated sketching it all afresh. I had to refrain totally from doing this, except that here and there I retouched some parts that didn't work in the sense of my original conception. Thus at times we really are speaking of shadows here, of a life that no longer exists; and furthermore, in some mildly annoying way we are speaking of a life that can lay no claims to conclusiveness. The faith that I nonetheless place in the durability of these little satires derives from a line of Goethe's, that may without forfeit of truth be modified to suit my purpose. So it reads: "In one thing done badly you can see the simile of all things done badly." This line offers a ray of hope that the critique of little errors may not be rendered obsolete, even in times when so much larger errors are being made.

Posthumous Papers
of a Living Author

Pictures

Flypaper

Tangle-foot flypaper is approximately fourteen inches long and eight inches wide; it is coated with a yellow poison paste and comes from Canada. When a fly lands on it—not so eagerly, more out of convention, because so many others are already there—it gets stuck at first by only the outermost joints of all its legs. A very quiet, disconcerting sensation, as though while walking in the dark we were to step on something with our naked soles, nothing more than a soft, warm, unavoidable obstruction, and yet something into which little by little the awesome human essence flows, recognized as a hand that just happens to be lying there, and with five ever more decipherable fingers, holds us tight.

Here they stand all stiffly erect, like cripples pretending to be normal, or like decrepit old soldiers (and a little bowlegged, the way you stand on a sharp edge). They hold themselves upright, gathering strength and pondering their position. After a few seconds they've come to a tactical decision and they begin to do what they can, to buzz and try to lift themselves. They continue this frantic effort until exhaustion makes them stop. Then they take a breather and try again. But the intervals grow ever longer. They stand there and I feel how helpless they are. Bewildering vapors rise from below. Their tongue gropes about like a tiny hammer. Their head is brown and hairy, as though made of a coconut, as manlike as an African idol. They twist forward and backward on their firmly fastened little legs, bend at the knees and lean forward like men trying to move a too heavy load: more tragic than the working man, truer as an athletic expression of the greatest exertion than Laocoön. And then comes the extraordinary moment when the imminent need of a second's relief wins out over the almighty instincts of self-preservation. It is the moment when the mountain climber because of the pain in his fingers willfully loosens his grip, when the man lost in the snow lays himself down like a child, when the hunted man stops dead with aching lungs. They no longer hold themselves up with all their might, but sink a little and at that moment appear totally human. Immediately they get stuck somewhere else, higher up on the leg, or behind, or at the tip of a wing.

When after a little while they've overcome the spiritual exhaustion and resume the fight for survival, they're trapped in an unfavorable position and their movements become unnatural. Then they lie down with outstretched hindlegs, propped up on their elbows and try to lift themselves. Or else seated on the ground, they rear up with outstretched arms like women who attempt in vain to wrest their hands free of a man's fists. Or they lie on their belly, with head and arms in front of them as though fallen while running, and they only still hold up their face. But the enemy is always passive and wins at just such desperate, muddled moments. A nothing, an *it* draws them in: so slowly that one can hardly follow, and usually with an abrupt acceleration at the very end, when the last inner breakdown overcomes them. Then, all of a sudden, they let themselves fall, forwards on their face, head over heels; or sideways with all legs collapsed; frequently also rolled on their side with their legs rowing to the rear. This is how they lie there. Like crashed planes with one wing reaching out into the air. Or like dead horses. Or with endless gesticulations of despair. Or like sleepers. Sometimes even the next day, one of them wakes up, gropes a while with one leg or flutters a wing. Sometimes such a movement sweeps over the lot, then all of them sink a little deeper into death. And only on the side, near their legsockets, is there some tiny wriggling organ that still lives a long time. It opens and closes, you can't describe it without a magnifying glass, it looks like a miniscule human eye that ceaselessly opens and shuts.

Monkey Island

In the Villa Borghese in Rome a tall tree stands without
bark or branches. It is as bald as a skull, pealed clean by sun
and water, and yellow as a skeleton. It stands erect without
roots and is dead, and, like a mast, is implanted in the
cement of an oval island the size of a small steamboat, and
separated from the kingdom of Italy by a smooth, concrete-
covered ditch. This ditch is just wide enough, and on the
outer side, just deep enough, so that a monkey could neither
climb through it nor jump over it. From the outside in, it
could probably be done, but not the other way around.

The trunk in the middle offers very good grips, and as
tourists like to say, is ideal for free and easy climbing. But
up on top, long, firm branches grow out horizontally; and
if you were to take off your shoes and socks and with
inward-hugging heels, with your soles pressed fast to the
rounded branch, and your hands grasping firmly, one in
front of the other, you'd have no trouble reaching the end
of one of these long, sun-soaked branches that stretch out
over the green, ostrich-feathered peaks of the pines.

This wonderful island is settled by three families of
varying size and number. About fifteen sinewy, nimble boys
and girls, all about the size of a four-year-old child, inhabit

the tree; while at the foot of the tree, in the only building on the island, a palace, the shape and size of a doghouse, a couple of far mightier monkeys live with a very small son. This is the island's royal couple and the crown prince. Never do the old ones wander far from home; like watchmen, motionless, they sit to the right and left of him and stare down their snouts into the distance. Only once every hour the king rouses himself and mounts the tree for a perambulating look around. Slowly he then steps along the boughs, and it doesn't seem that he cares to notice how reverentially and distrustfully everyone shrinks back, and— to avoid a stir—they slink over sideways till the end of the branch permits no further retreat, and nothing but a perilous leap down to the hard concrete is left. So the king strides the length of the boughs, one after the other, and the most acute attentiveness cannot decipher whether all the while his face evinces the discharge of a ruler's duty or a survey of the grounds. Meanwhile, on the palace roof the crown prince sits alone, for astonishingly his mother also always departs at the same time, and through his thin, wide, stick-out ears the sun shines coral-red. Seldom can one see a thing so dumb and pathetic, and yet so much encompassed by an invisible dignity, as this young monkey. One after the other, the tree monkeys, who were chased to the ground, file past him, and could easily twist off his skinny neck with a single grip: they're in an awful mood, but they make a wide detour around him and display all the reverence and reserve that his family is due.

It takes a long time to notice that aside from these beings who live such a well-ordered life, still others inhabit the island. Driven from the surface and the air, a large population of little monkeys live in the ditch. If one of them even shows his face on the island above, he is chased by the tree monkeys back into the ditch, under severe reprisals. At feeding time the little ones must sit timidly to the side, and only when the others are full and mostly at rest up in the tree, are they permitted to sneak over to the crumbs. They're not even allowed to touch what's thrown to them. A nasty boy or a tricky girl are often just waiting for the chance. Though with a wink they may feign indigestion, they carefully slip down from their perch, as soon as they notice that the little ones are having too good a time. Those few who dared climb up onto the island are already scurrying screaming back into the ditch; and they mingle with the others; and the howling outcry begins: And now they all press together, so that a single surface of hair and flesh and mad, dark eyes swell up against the outer wall like water in a tipped-over tub. The persecutor, however, only walks along the edge and shoves the wave of shuddering terror back away from himself. Thereupon the little black faces stir and they throw up their arms and stretch out their palms in supplication before the evil foreign eye that gazes down from the edge. And soon this gaze attaches itself to one individual; he shoves backwards and forwards, and five others do it with him, who can't yet make out which one of them is the target of this long look; but the weak, fear-crippled mass of monkeys does not budge. Then the long, indifferent gaze nails its arbitrary victim; and at last it's completely impossible to control oneself any longer, not to show either too much or too little fear: and from one moment to the next the lapse of self-control swells, while one soul digs into another, till the hate is there, and the crack gives way, and without shame or poise a creature whines under torture. With the release of a scream, the others rush apart on down the ditch; they flicker dimly about like the damned souls in the flames of purgatory, and gather chattering cheerfully as far from the scene as possible.

When it's all over with, the persecutor climbs with a feathery grip up the big tree to its highest branch, strides out to the very end of the branch, peacefully seats himself, and serious, erect, and ever so long, he stays like that without rousing. The beam of his glance glides over the Pincio and the Villa Borghese; and where it leaves the gardens behind, there beneath it lies the great yellow city, over which, still swathed in the green shimmering cloud of the tree top, it floats, oblivious to all, suspended in midair.

Fishermen on the Baltic

On the beach they've dug out a little pit with their hands, and from a sack of black earth they're pouring in fat earthworms; the loose black earth and the mass of worms make for an obscure, moldy, enticing ugliness in the clean white sand. Beside this they place a very tidy looking wooden chest is placed. It looks like a long, not particularly wide drawer or counting board, and is full of clean yarn; and on the other side of the pit another such, but empty, drawer is placed.

The hundred hooks attached to the yarn in the one drawer are neatly arranged on the end of a small iron pole and are now being unfastened one after the other and laid in the empty drawer, the bottom of which is filled with nothing but clean wet sand. A very tidy operation. In the meantime, however, four long, lean and strong hands oversee the process as carefully as nurses to make sure that each hook gets a worm.

The men who do this crouch two by two on knees and heels, with mighty, bony backs, long, kindly faces, and pipes in their mouths. They exchange incomprehensible words that flow forth as softly as the motion of their hands. One of them takes up a fat earthworm with two fingers, tears it into three pieces with the same two fingers of the other hand, as easily and exactly as a shoemaker snips off the paper band after he's taken the measurement; the other one then presses these squirming pieces calmly and carefully onto each hook. This having been accomplished, the worms are then doused with water and laid in neat, little beds, one next to the other, in the drawer with the soft sand, where they can die without immediately loosing their freshness.

It is a quiet, delicate activity, whereby the coarse fishermen's fingers step softly as on tiptoes. You have to pay close attention. In fair weather the dark blue sky arches above, and the seagulls circle high over the land like white swallows.

Inflation

Once there was a better time, when you rode a wood-stiff pony pedantically ever returning around the same circle, and with a short rod poked for copper rings held still by a wooden arm. That time is gone. These days the fishermen's boys drink champagne mixed with cognac. And little swings hang in a circle on four times thirty little iron chains, one circle on the inside and one outside, so that as you fly side by side, you grab each other by hand, leg, or apron and shriek fiendishly. This carousel stands on the little square with the memorial for the fallen soldiers; next to the linden tree where the geese like to roost. It has a motor that revs up at the right time, and chalk-white spotlights over many little warm lights. If in the darkness you happen to grope your way closer, the wind'll fling shreds of music, lights, girls' voices, and laughter at you. The orchestrion cries with a sob. The iron chains screech. You fly round in the circle, but also, if you wish, upward or downward, outward or inward, back to back or between the legs. The boys spur on their swings and pinch the girls where they can feel it, or tear the shrieking damsels along with them; and the girls also grab each other in flight, and then in pairs they scream just as loud as if one of them were a boy. So they all swing through the cone of light into the darkness and are suddenly thrust back into the light; paired off anew, with foreshortened limbs and black mouths, whizzing, bedazzled bundles of clothing, they fly on their backs or on their bellies or obliquely toward heaven or hell. After a very short while of this wild gallop, the orchestrion quickly falls back into a trot, like an old circus horse, then it paces and soon stands still. The man with the pewter plate makes the rounds, but you stay seated or maybe switch girls. And unlike in the city, no ever-changing crowd frequents the carousel the few days it's around; because here always the same ones fly from the advent of darkness on, for two to three hours, all eight or fourteen days, up until the man with the pewter plate grows tired of it all and one morning has moved on.

Can a Horse Laugh?

An acclaimed psychologist wrote: ". . . for animals don't know how to laugh or smile."

This emboldens me to admit that I once saw a horse laugh. Till now I assumed that this was nothing special, and I didn't dare make a big deal of it; but if it is such a rarity, I will gladly elaborate.

Well, it was before the war; it could be that since then horses no longer laugh. The horse was tied to a sedge fence that surrounded a little yard. The sky was dark blue. The air was particularly mild, even though it was February. And in contrast to this heavenly calm, there was no human presence: to make a long story short, I found myself near Rome, on a country road just outside the city limits, on the border between the city's humble outskirts and the first fringe of the peasant Campagna.

The horse also was a Campagna horse: young and graceful, of that shapely, tiny breed with nothing pony-like about it, on the back of which, however, a big rider looks like a grown-up on a little doll's stool. It was being brushed by a fun-loving stable boy, the sun shone on its hide, and it was ticklish under the shoulders. Now a horse has, so to speak, four shoulders, and perhaps for that reason, is twice as ticklish as a man; besides which, this horse also seemed to have a particularly sensitive spot on the inside of each of its haunches, and every time it was touched there, it could hardly keep from laughing.

As soon as the currycomb came close, it drew back its ears, became uneasy, wanted to edge over with its mouth, and when it couldn't do this, bared its teeth. But the comb marched merrily on, stroke after stroke, and the lips revealed ever more of the teeth, while the ears lay themselves farther and farther back, and the horse tipped from one leg to the other.

And suddenly it started to laugh. It flashed its teeth. With its muzzle it tried as hard as it could to push away the boy who was tickling it; just like a peasant girl would do with her hand, and without trying to bite him. It also attempted to turn itself around and to shove him away with its entire body. But the stable boy held the advantage. And when with the currycomb he arrived in the vicinity of its shoulders, the horse could no longer control itself; it shifted from leg to leg, shivered all over, and pulled back the gums from its teeth as far as it could. For a few seconds then, it behaved just like a man tickled so much that he can't even laugh anymore.

The learned sceptic will object here, that the horse couldn't laugh after all. One must admit to the validity of his objection, insofar as, of the two, the one who whinnied with laughter was the stable boy. The ability to whinny with laughter seems in fact to be exclusively a human talent. But nonetheless, the two of them were obviously playing together, and as soon as they started it all over again from the beginning, there could be no doubt that the horse wanted to laugh and was already anticipating the sequence of sensations.

So learned doubt defines the limitations of the beast's ability, that it cannot laugh at jokes.

This, however, should not always be held against the horse.

Awakening

I shoved the curtain aside—the soft night! A gentle darkness lies in the window cutout of the hard room darkness like the water surface in a square basin. I don't really see it at all, but it's like in the summer when the water's as warm as the air and your hand hangs out of the boat. It is going on six o'clock, November 1st.

God woke me up. I shot up out of sleep. I had absolutely no other reason to wake up. I was torn out like a page from a book. The moon's crescent lies delicate as a golden eyebrow on the blue page of night.

But on the morning side at the other window it's getting green. Parrot-feathery. The pale reddish stripes of sunrise, they too are already streaking the sky, but everything's still green, blue and silent. I jump back to the other window: is the moon still there? She's there, as though in the deepest hour of night's secret. So convinced is she of the effectiveness of her magic, like an actress on stage. (There's nothing stranger than to step out of the morning streets into the illusion of a theatre rehearsal.) The street's already pulsing to the left, and to the right the moon is in rehearsal.

I discover strange fellows, the smoke stacks. In groups of three, five, seven, and sometimes alone, they stand up on the rooftops; like trees in the landscape. Space winds like a river around them and into the deep. An owl slips past them on its way home; it was probably a crow or a pigeon. The houses stand helter-skelter; curious contours, steep sloping walls; not at all arranged by streets. The rod on the roof with the thirty-six porcelain heads and the twelve stretched wires, which I count without comprehension, stands as a completely inexplicable secret structure up against the early morning sky. I'm wide awake now, but wherever I look, my eyes glide over pentagons, heptagons, and steep prisms: so who am I? The amphora on the roof with its cast-iron flame, ridiculous pineapple by day, vulgar, disgusting thing—now in this solitude it soothes the heart, like a fresh trace of humanity.

At last two legs come through the night. The step of two woman legs in my ear: I don't want to look. My ear stands like a gateway on the street. Never will I be so at one with a woman as with this unknown figure whose steps disappear ever deeper in my ear.

Then two women. The one sordidly slinking along, the other stamping with the disregard of age. I look down. Black. The clothes of old women have a form all their own. These two are bound for church. At this hour the soul has long since been taken into custody, and so I won't have anything more to do with it.

Sheep, As Seen in Another Light

As to the history of sheep: Today man views the sheep as stupid. But God loved it. He repeatedly compared man with sheep. Is it possible that God was completely wrong?

As to the psychology of sheep: The finely chiseled expression of exalted consciousness is not unlike the look of stupidity.

On the heath near Rome: They had the long faces and the delicate skulls of martyrs. Their black stockings and hoods against the white fur reminded of morbid monks and fanatics.

When they rummaged through the low, sparse grass, their lips trembled nervously and scattered the timbre of a quivering steel string over the earth. Joined in chorus, their voices rang out like the lamentations of prelates in the cathedral. But when many of them sang together, they formed a men's, women's, and children's choir. In soft swells they lifted and lowered their voices; it was like a wandering train in the darkness, struck every other second by light, and the children's voices then stood on an ever-returning hill, while the men strode through the valley. Day and night rolled a thousand times faster through their song and drove the earth onwards to its end. Sometimes a solitary voice flung itself up or tumbled down in fear of damnation. Heaven's clouds were recreated in the white ringlets of their hair. These are age-old catholic animals, religious companions of mankind.

Once again in the South: Man is twice as big as usual in their midst and reaches like a church spire up toward heaven. Beneath our feet the earth was brown, and the grass like scratched-in grey-green stripes. The sun shone heavy on the sea as on a lead mirror. Boats were busy fishing as in Saint Peter's time. The cape swung the view like a running board up toward heaven and broke off into the dark yellow and white sea as in wandering Odysseus' day.

Everywhere: When man approaches, sheep are timid and stupid; they have known the beatings and stones of his insolence. But if he stands stock still and stares into the distance, they forget about him. They stick their heads together then, ten or fifteen of them, and form the spokes of a wheel, with the big, heavy center-point of heads and the otherwise-colored spokes of their backs. They press their skulls tightly together. This is how they stand, and the wheel that they form won't budge for hours. They don't seem to want to feel anything but the wind and the sun, and between their foreheads, the seconds striking out eternity that beats in their blood and signals from head to head like the hammering of prisoners on prison walls.

Sarcophagus Cover

Somewhere to the rear of the Pincio, or already in Villa Borghese, two sarcophagus covers of a common sort of stone lie out in the open between the bushes. They constitute no rare treasure, they're just lying around. Stretched out on top of them, the couple who once as a final memento had themselves copied in stone, are at rest. One sees many such sarcophagus covers in Rome; but in no museum and in no church do they make such an impression as here under the trees, where as though on a picnic, the figures stretched themselves out, and seem just to have awakened from a little sleep that lasted two thousand years.

They've propped themselves up on their elbows and are eyeing each other. All that's missing between them is the basket of cheese, fruit, and wine.

The woman wears a hairdo of little curls—any minute now she'll arrange them according to the latest fashion from the time before she fell asleep. And they're smiling at each other; a long, a very long smile. You look away: And still they go on smiling.

This faithful, proper, middle class, beloved look has lasted centuries; it was sent forth in ancient Rome and crosses your glance today.

23

Don't be surprised that even in front of you it endures,that they don't look away or lower their eyes: this doesn't make them stone-like, but rather all the more human.

Rabbit Catastrophe

No doubt the lady had just the day before stepped out of the window display of a department store; her doll's face was so dainty, you would have liked to stir it up with a teaspoon just to see it in motion. But you yourself wore shoes with showy, slick, honeycomb soles, and knickers as if tailor-made to measure. At least you delighted in the wind. It pressed the dress against the lady and made a sorry little skeleton of her, a dumb little face with a tiny mouth. Of course she feigned a dauntless look for the benefit of the observer.

Little jackrabbits live unawares beside the white pleats and the thin-as-teacup skirts. Dark green like laurel, the island's epic surrounds them. Flocks of seagulls nest in the heath hollows like snow blossoms swept by the wind. The little, white fur-collared lady's miniature, long-haired terrier is rummaging through the bush, its nose a finger's width above the ground; far and wide there's no other dog to sniff out on the island, there's nothing here but the vast romance of many little, unknown paths that crisscross the island. In this solitude the dog grows huge, a hero. Aroused, he barks dagger-sharp and bares his teeth like some sea monster. Hopelessly the lady purses her lips to whistle; the wind tears the tiny attempt at a sound from her mouth.

I've already covered glacier paths with just such an impetuous fox-terrier; we humans smoothly on our skis, him bleeding, his belly collapsed, cut up by the ice, and nonetheless enlivened by a wild, insatiable bliss. Now this one here has picked up the scent of something; his legs gallop like little sticks, his bark becomes a sob. It's amazing at this moment how much such a flat, sea-swept island can remind one of the great glens and highlands of the mountains. The dunes, yellow as skulls and smoothed by the wind, sit like craggy peaks. Between them and the sky lies the emptiness of unfinished creation. Light doesn't shine on this and that, but spills out over everything as from an accidentally overturned bucket.

One is always astonished that animals inhabit this solitude. They take on a mysterious aspect; their little, soft, wooly and feathery breasts shelter the spark of life. It's a little jackrabbit that the terrier is chasing. A little, weather-beaten, mountain type; he'll never catch him, I bet. A memory from geography class comes to mind: island? Are we actually standing here on the peak of a high ocean mountain? We ten or fifteen idly observant vacationers, in our colorful madhouse jackets, as the fashion prescribes. I change my mind again and say to myself, it would all be nothing but inhuman loneliness: bewildered as a horse that has thrown its rider, is the earth wherever man is in the minority; moreover, nature proves itself to be not at all healthy, downright mentally disturbed in the high mountains and on tiny islands. But to our amazement, the distance between the dog and the hare has diminished; the terrier is catching up, we've never seen such a thing: a dog catching up with a hare! This will be the first great triumph of the canine world! Enthusiasm spurs on the hunter, his breath sobs in gulps, there's no longer any doubt that in a matter of seconds he will have caught his prey. The hare pirouettes. Here I recognize in a certain softness, because the crucial cut is missing in its turn, that it's not a grown rabbit at all, but a harelet, a rabbit child.

I feel my heart; the dog turned too and hasn't lost more than fifteen steps; in a matter of seconds the rabbit catastrophe will occur. The child hears the hunter hot on its tail, it is tired. I want to jump between them, but it takes such a long time for the will to slide down my pants pleats and into my smooth soles; or perhaps the resistance was already in my head. Twenty steps in front of me—I would have had to have imagined it, if the baby rabbit hadn't stopped in despair and held its neck out to the hunter. He dug in with his teeth, swung it a few times back and forth, then flung it on its side and buried his mouth two or three times in its breast and belly.

I looked up. Laughing, heated faces stood around. It suddenly felt like four in the morning after you've danced through the night. The first one of us to wake up from this blood lust was the little terrier. He let go, squinted diffidently to the side, pulled back; after a few steps he fell into a short, timid gallop, as though he expected a stone to come flying after him. But the rest of us were motionless and disturbed. The insipid air of cannibalistic platitudes hovered round us, like "fight for survival" or "the brutality of nature." Such thoughts, like the shoals of an ocean bottom, though risen from great depths, are shallow. I would have loved to go back and slap the silly little lady. This was a noble sentiment, but not a good one, and so I kept still and thereby joined the general uncertainty and the swelling silence. But finally a tall, well-to-do gentleman picked up the hare with both his hands, showed its wounds to the onlookers and carried the corpse, swiped from the dog, like a little coffin into the kitchen of the nearby hotel. The man was the first to step out of the unfathomable and had Europe's firm ground beneath his feet.

The Mouse

This miniscule story, that in fact is nothing but a punch line, a single tiny tip of a tale, and not a story at all, happened during the first World War. On the Swiss Fodora Vedla Alps, more than three thousand feet above inhabited ground, and still much farther off the beaten track: there in peacetime somebody had put up a bench.

This bench stood untouched, even by the war. In a wide, right hollow. The shots sailed over it. Silent as ships, like schools of fish. They struck far back where nothing and no one was, and for months, with an iron perseverance, ravaged an innocent precipice. No one knew why anymore. An error of the art of war? A whim of the war gods? This bench was abandoned by the war. And all day long, from way up in its infinite altitude, the sun sent light to keep it company.

Whoever sat on this bench sat firm. The moon rose no more. Your legs slept a separate sleep, like men who, having flung themselves down close together, exhausted, forgot each other in the same instant. Your own breath was strange; it became an occurrence of nature; no, not "nature's breath," but rather: if you noticed at all that you were breathing—this steady, mindless motion of the breast!—

something of man's swooning at the blue colossus of the atmosphere, something like a pregnancy.

The grass all around was left over from the previous year; snow bleached and ugly; bloodless, as though a huge boulder had been rolled away. There were innumerable humps and hollows near and far, knee-high timber, and alpine meadow. From this motionless turmoil, from this decayed, yellow-green frothy break of ground, again and again your glance was flung ever upwards at the high, red, overhanging cliff which sliced off the landscape in front, and from which your glance retreated, shattered into a hundred vistas. That jagged cliff was not all that high, yet above it loomed nothing but empty light. It was so savage and so inhumanly beautiful, as we imagine in the ages of the creation.

Near the bench, which was seldom visited, a little mouse had dug itself a system of running trenches. Mouse-deep, with holes to disappear and elsewhere reappear. She scurried around in circles, stood still, then scurried round again. A terrible silence emanated from the sullen atmosphere. The human hand dropped off the armrest. An eye, as small and black as the head of a spinning needle, turned to look. And for an instant you had such a strange twisted feeling, that you really no longer knew: was it this tiny, living black eye that turned? Or the stirring of the mountains' huge immobility? You just didn't know anymore: had you been touched by the will of the world, or by the will of this mouse, that glowed out of a little, lonesome eye? You didn't know: was war still raging or had eternity won the day?

So you might have continued at length to ramble on about something you felt you could not know; but that's all for this little story, that had already come to an end every time you tried to end it.

Clearhearing

I went to bed earlier than usual, feeling a slight cold, I might even have a fever. I am staring at the ceiling, or perhaps it's the reddish curtain over the balcony door of our hotel room that I see; it's hard to distinguish.

As soon as I'd finished with it, you too started to undress. I'm waiting. I can only hear you.

Incomprehensible, all the walking up and down; in this corner of the room, in that. You come over to lay something on your bed; I don't look up, but what could it be? In the meantime, you open the closet, put something in or take something out; I hear it close again. You lay hard, heavy objects on the table, others on the marble top of the commode. You are forever in motion. Then I recognize the familiar sounds of hair being undone and brushed. Then swirls of water in the sink. Even before that, clothes being shed; now again; it's just incomprehensible to me how many clothes you take off. Finally you've slipped out of your shoes. But now your stockings slide as constantly back and forth over the soft carpet as your shoes did before. You pour water into glasses; three, four times without stopping, I can't even guess why. In my imagination I have long since given up on anything imaginable, while you evidently keep finding new things to do in the realm of reality. I hear you slip into your nightgown. But you aren't finished yet and won't be for a while. Again there are a hundred little actions. I know that you're rushing for my sake; so all this must be absolutely necessary, part of your most intimate I, and like the mute motion of animals from morning till evening, you reach out with countless gestures, of which you're unaware, into a region where you've never heard my step!

By coincidence I feel it all, because I have a fever and am waiting for you.

Slovenian Village Funeral

My room was strange. Pompeian red with Turkish curtains; the furniture had rents and seams in which the dust gathered like tiny boulder beds and bands. It was a delicate dust, unreal rocks in miniature; but it was so very simply there, so uninvolved in any action, that it reminded of the great solitude of the mountains, bathed only by the rising and falling of the flood of light and darkness. In those days I had many such experiences.

The first time I set foot in the house, it was completely saturated with the stench of dead mice. Into the shared antechamber that separated my room from that of the teachers, they threw everything that they no longer loved or cared to keep: artificial flowers, food scraps, fruit peels, and torn dirty laundry no longer worth the effort of being cleaned. Even my servant complained when I asked him to clean it up; and yet one of the teachers was prettier than an angel, and her sister was gentler than a mother, and every day she painted her sister's cheeks with naive rose colors, so that her face would be as beautiful as the peasant madonna in the little church. They were both loved by the little schoolgirls who came to visit; and I myself learned to appreciate this, when once I was sick and they gave me to feel of their goodness like warm herb cushions. But once during the day, when I entered their room to ask for something, for they were my landladies, both of them lay in bed, and as soon as I turned to leave, they jumped out from under the blankets fully dressed and ready to help; they even kept their filthy street shoes on in bed.

This then was the apartment in which I stood as I watched the funeral; a fat woman had died, who had lived diagonally across from my window on the other side of the wide, and here somewhat bulging, thoroughfare. In the morning the carpenter's boys brought the coffin; it was winter, and they brought it on a little handsled, and because it was a lovely morning, they slid down the street with their spiked shoes, and the big black box behind them jumped from side to side. Everyone who watched had the feeling, what handsome boys they were, and all waited expectantly to see if the sled would topple over or not.

But by afternoon the last of the escort already stood in front of the house: top hats and fur caps, fashionable haberdashery and winter kerchiefs dark against the light snow-grey of the sky. And the priests in black and red, with crenulated white shirts on top, came walking across the snow. And a young, big, shaggy brown dog chased after them and barked as though at a car. And if one may be permitted to say so, the dog did not express an altogether false perception; for, in fact, at that moment there was nothing so much holy or even human about the approaching figures, as simply the heavy motion of the mechanical side of their existence sweeping over the slippery ice-slick that covered the street.

But then the mood turned suddenly divine. A quiet bass intoned a wonderfully soft sad song, in which I understood only the foreign words for sweet Mary; a baritone, shimmering light-brown like chestnuts, joined in, and still another voice; and a tenor soared over all the rest, while women with black kerchiefs flowed out of the house in an unending stream; the candles burned pale golden against the winter sky and all the implements sparkled. One would have

34

wanted to cry then, and for no other reason than that one already was a human being over thirty.

Perhaps also just a little bit because the boys poked and punched each other behind the party of mourners. Or because the upstanding young man, to whom the dog belonged, stared motionlessly over everyone's head at the holy service, and you couldn't say why. Everything was just so full of facts that didn't quite sit right, as in a china cabinet. And to tell the truth, I could hardly control myself, and didn't know where to turn, when by coincidence, in the midst of the crowd, I once again noticed that the deeply touched young man held one hand behind his back and his big brown dog began to play with it. Playfully he bit at it and tried to wake it up with his warm tongue. Impatiently I waited to see what would happen. And finally, after a long time, while the whole of the young man's body remained frozen in unsettled exaltation, the hand freed itself behind his back and began playing with the dog's mouth, without the man's knowing it.

This once again made my soul regain its balance, without any real reason. At that time, in those surroundings where I forced myself to hold out, my soul slipped easily into chaos or order at the slightest upset. I was shot through with eagerness and anxiety in anticipation of the hand-shake that my housemates would offer me after the funeral, together with a little glass of their suspicious homebrew and a few fitting words that were not to be contradicted: maybe, that misfortune brings people closer together, or something like that.

Maidens and Heroes

How lovely are you servant girls with your peasant legs and those peaceful eyes, about which you just can't tell, do they wonder about everything or about nothing?! You lead the master's dog by the leash like a cow on the line. Are you thinking about how the bells back in the village are ringing now, or are you thinking that the movie's about to begin? The only sure thing is that you sense in some secret way that more men live in between the corners of the city than in all your country, and you move at every moment through this male dominion, even if it doesn't belong to you, as though through a farm field that brushes up against your skirts.

But are you aware, while your eyes pretend to know nothing, that it's a man you lead by the leash? Or don't you realize at all that Lux is a man, that Wolf and Amri are men? A thousand arrows pierce their hearts at every tree and lamppost. Men of their breed have left as their mark the dagger-sharp smell of ammonia, as though they'd stuck a sword into a tree; combats, brotherhoods, braveries and desire, the whole heroic world of man unfolds itself to their sniffing imagination! How they lift a leg with the noble poise of a warrior's salute, or the heroic sweep of a beer-glass-toasting arm at a drinking bout! With what earnest do they carry out their duty, that is surely a consecrated drink-offering like no other! And you girls? So thoughtlessly you drag these dogs after you. Tug on the leash; don't grant them time, without even looking back at them. It's a sight that'd make one want to throw stones at you.

Brothers! On three legs Lucky or Wolf hop after the girls; too proud, too injured in their pride to howl for help; incapable of any other protest than headstrong and stubbornly, in desperate farewell, not to let the fourth leg drop, while the leash drags them ever onwards. What inner dog-dismay must come of such moments, what desperate neurasthenic complexes lie buried there! And the main thing: do you sense the sad comradely look he casts at you, when you pass such a scene? In his way, he even loves the soul of these thoughtless girls. They aren't heartless; their heart would be moved if they knew what was happening. But they just don't know. And aren't they for that very reason so ravishing, these hard-hearted things, because they know nothing at all about us? Thus speaks the dog. They will never understand our world!

Boardinghouse Nevermore

There was once a German boardinghouse in Rome.
(Though besides this one there were also many others.) In
those days in Italy, the German boardinghouse was a
specific term that encompassed many varied and singular
types. Even today I shudder when I think back to another
one where I once lived; everything was so impeccable there
you wanted to cry. But it wasn't like that at the boardinghouse that I am talking about. When I first stepped into the
office and asked for the man of the house, his mother
replied: "Oh, he can't make it now; it's his corns, you
know!" I'd like to call him Mr. Nevermore. His mother,
Mrs. Nevermore, was a matron of mighty proportions
whose flesh had slipped back a bit over the years, so that her
corset traced an uneven ring in the air around her. Over her
corset a blouse was spanned; somehow she reminded me of
an overturned, abandoned umbrella, the kind you sometimes find in vacant lots. Her hair, as far as I could tell, was
never combed between Easter and October, that is, outside
the tourist season. During the season it seemed to be white.
Another one of her idiosyncracies involved a skirt with an
unusually long slit that stayed open from top to bottom
when it was hot. Perhaps it was cooler like that, or perhaps

it was a special feature of the house. For even Laura, the chambermaid, who served at table, put on a clean blouse which, for this express purpose, closed at the back; but during the time I spent in Rome only the bottom two of all the hooks were ever done, so that above this Laura's camisole and also her lovely back were presented as on a chalice.

Still they were outstanding hosts, the Nevermores; their old-fashioned, luxurious rooms were well kept, and whatever they cooked had a special touch. During meals Mr. Nevermore himself stood by as head waiter beside the serving table and supervised the staff, which consisted, however, only of Laura. Once I heard him complain to her: "Mr. Meier fetched a spoon and the salt for himself!" Frightened, Laura whispered: "Did he say anything?" And with the quiet reserve of a royal steward, Mr. Nevermore replied: "Mr. Meier never says anything!" To such pinnacles of his profession could he raise himself. He was, so far as I can remember, tall, lean, and bald, with a watery look in his eyes, and a prickly stubble on his cheeks that slowly shifted upward and downward when he bent over toward a guest with a bowl to discreetly point out something particularly delicious. They simply had their own ways, the Nevermores.

And I jotted down all these little details because even then I had the feeling that there will never be the likes of such an establishment again. I certainly don't mean to imply that there was something particularly rare or precious about the place; it merely had something to do with a coincidence of time, a phenomenon difficult to describe. If twenty clocks are hanging on one wall and you suddenly look at them, every pendulum is in a different place; they all tell the same time and yet don't, and the real time flows somewhere in between. This can have an uncanny effect. All of us who at the time boarded at the Pension Nevermore had our own particular reasons for being there; we all had something more to do in Rome than just spending time, and since the summer heat only permitted us to carry out a tiny portion of our task each day, we met each other again and again at our home away from home. There was, for instance, the little old Swiss gentleman; he was here to represent the interests of a Protestant sect, not much larger than himself, a group that wanted to build a Protestant chapel in papal Rome, of all places. Despite the burning sun, he always wore a black suit; on the second vest button from the top his watch chain was fastened, and just a little lower down hung a black medallion in which a golden cross was set. His beard really sat to the right and left of him; it sprouted so thinly from his chin that you only noticed it from a distance. In the proximity of his cheeks this beard completely lost itself, just like on his upper lip, which was naturally beardless. The hair on this old gentleman's head was blond-gray and unbelievably soft; and his complexion might well have been rosy, but since it was white, it was as white as freshly fallen snow, in which a pair of gold-rimmed glasses are lying. Once when we were all chatting in the parlor, this old gentleman said to Mme. Gervais: "Do you know what you need? You need a king in France!"

—I was surprised and wanted to come to Mme. Gervais' assistance: "But aren't you Swiss and a republican yourself!?" I insisted. And here the little man radiated out over his golden glasses and answered us: "Oh, that is quite another matter! We've been a republic for six hundred years, and not for forty-five!" So much for the Swiss gentleman who was building a Protestant church in Rome.

With her sweet smile, Mme. Gervais responded: "If there were no diplomats and newspapers, we would have eternal peace." "*Excellent, vraiment excellent!*" the old gentleman, pacified again, agreed and nodded with a titter that sounded so very refined and unnatural, as though he had a young goat trapped in his throat; he had to lift one leg from the ground to lean back in his easy chair toward Mme. Gervais.

But only Mme. Gervais could offer such sage responses. The first time I saw her, the profile of her delicate Titushead on her slender neck, adorned with a dainty ear, stood out in relief against the dining room window, in front of which she sat like a rose-colored stone set in sky-blue silk. Her fastidious hands equipped with knife and fork, her arms drawn in upon themselves, she shaved the skin off the body of a peach she had speared. Her favorite words were: *ignoble, mal élevé, grand luxe,* and *très maniaque.* She also often said *digestion* and *digestif.* Mme. Gervais liked to tell how she, the good Catholic, was once in a Protestant church in Paris on the emperor's birthday. "And I assure you," she added, "it was much more refined than ours. Much simpler. None of that undignified pomp!"—That is what Mme. Gervais was like.

She argued in favor of a German-French accord, because her husband was a hotelier. More accurately, he was making a hotel career: one needs to experience everything, dining room, bar, room service, office. "Just as an engineer needs to work the vice!" she put it. She was an enlightened woman. She was enraged at the memory of how a black prince, a complete gentleman, was snubbed by Americans at a Paris hotel. "So he just went like this!" she demonstrated, enacting a delightfully disdainful turn of the lips. The classical, noble ideals of humanity, internationalism, and human dignity combined in her with the precepts of the hotel business to create a perfect unity. She did like to add, however, that as a girl she took automobile trips with her parents, and that she went here and there in the company of this or that attaché or consular secretary, or that her acquaintance, the Marquise So-and-so, had said this and that. But when talking of the hotel business she made no less of a to-do that a friend of her husband, in an establishment that prohibited tips, took in 800 Deutsch marks in tips a month, whereas her husband, in a place that permitted tips, made only 600 Deutsch marks. She always had fresh flowers with her and traveled with a dozen doilies, with the aid of which she made a little home of every hotel room. There she welcomed her husband when he was not working, and she had an arrangement with Laura, who would wash her stockings for her as soon as she took them off. She was in fact a brave woman.

Once I noticed that her little mouth could also appear fleshy, although the overall effect of her person was that of a somewhat elongated, extremely delicate angel; if you looked closely, her cheeks also rose much too high above her nose when she laughed; but strangely enough, though I found her less pretty thereafter, we spoke more seriously with each other from that point on. She told me of the sadness of her childhood, of her early and lengthy illnesses and of the torments she had to endure from the moods of a paralytic, invalid stepfather. Once she even confessed to me that it was for this reason that she married her husband without loving him. Just because it was time to take care of herself, she said: *"Sans enthousiasme, vraiment sans enthousiasme!"* But this she only confessed to me a day before my departure: she always knew just the right thing to say, and addressed her listeners from the depths of her soul.

I would like to be able to say something similar about the lady from Wiesbaden, who likewise belonged to our household; but, unfortunately, I have forgotten a lot about her, and the little that I do remember leads me to believe that the rest would not suit my intention. The only thing I still recall is that she used to wear a skirt with vertical stripes, so that she looked like a high wooden latice on top of which an unpleated white blouse hung. When she spoke, it was invariably to contradict, and this usually happened in approximately the following manner: someone said, for instance, that Ottavina was beautiful. "Yes"—she immediately added—"a noble Roman type." Meanwhile she looked at you with such certainty, that for the sake of preserving world order, you had to correct her, whether you wanted to or not; for Ottavina, the chambermaid, was from Tuscany. "Yes"—she replied—"from Tuscany. But a Roman type! All Roman women have noses attached directly to the brow!" Now Ottavina was not only from Tuscany, but she also did not have a nose attached directly to her brow; nonetheless, the lady from Wiesbaden possessed such a lively spirit that a preconceived notion always popped out of her head simply because her other preconceived notions elbowed it out. I am afraid she was an unhappy woman. And perhaps she was not a woman at all, but a girl.

She had traveled by boat around Africa and wanted to visit Japan. Apropos of this, she told of a girlfriend who had drunk seven glasses of beer and smoked forty cigarettes, and she called her a swell chum. When she talked like this, her face looked terribly dissolute, with too much skin and crooked slits for a mouth, nose, and eyes; you thought at the least that she smoked opium. But as soon as she no longer felt herself observed, she had a perfectly proper face that stuck in the other like little Tom Thumb in seven-league boots. Her highest ideal was the lion hunt, and she asked us all if we thought one needed a great deal of strength to go on one? Courage—she said—of courage she had plenty, but was she also up to the hardships? Her nephew was trying to talk her into it because he would just love to be taken along; but for such a twenty-two-year-old rascal it was a different matter altogether, was it not? The good world-traveling aunt indeed! I am convinced that under the African sun she will give her nephew a good strong slap on the shoulder, and that the lion will slip away, as did Mme. Gervais and I whenever we got the chance.

Then I sometimes snuck over to Mrs. Nevermore's office or slipped down the hallway in search of Ottavina. I could just as well have cast a glance at the stars in heaven, but Ottavina was more beautiful. She was the second chambermaid, a nineteen-year-old peasant girl who had a husband and a little son at home; she was the most beautiful woman I have ever seen. Let no one tell me there are many different beauties, beauty of many types and degrees: I know all that. In fact, I never even held much by Ottavina's type of beauty; it was Raphael's type, to which I even have an aversion: but despite this beauty, what overpowered my eye was Ottavina's beauty! Fortunately, I can permit myself to say that for those who have never seen the like, it is impossible to describe. How revolting are the words harmony, symmetry, perfection, noble bearing! We have stuffed them so full of meaning, they stand before us like fat women on tiny feet and cannot even move. But once you have seen real harmony and perfection, you are astounded how natural it is. It is down to earth. It flows like a stream, not at all evenly, with the unabashed self-regard of nature, without straining for grandeur or perfection. If I say about Ottavina that she was big, strong, aristocratic, and elegant, I have the feeling that these words were borrowed from other people. She was big, but no less graceful. Strong, but in no way staid. Aristocratic without any loss of originality. At once a goddess and the second chambermaid. I never succeeded in speaking with the nineteen-year-old Ottavina, because she found my broken Italian unsuitable, and to everything I said, responded only with a very polite yes or no; but I think I worshipped her. Of course I don't even know for sure, because with Ottavina, everything meant something else. I did not desire her, I suffered no loss, I did not swoon; quite the contrary, every time I saw her, I tried to make myself as inconspicuous as a mortal who has stumbled into the company of the gods. She could smile without a wrinkle forming on her face. I imagined her in a man's arms in no other way than with that smile and a soft blush that spread out over her like a cloud, behind which she escaped the onslaught of desire.

Ottavina did after all have a legitimate son, and often without waiting for her, I slipped off to old Mrs. Nevermore's office to attempt in conversation with the old lady to re-establish my equilibrium with reality. When she moved through the room, she let her arms hang down, with the backs of her hands facing forward; she had the wide back and belly of a matron who no longer attempted to improve upon life. If, driven by the need to know, you asked her whether her black cat Michette was in fact a he or a she, she looked at you thoughtfully and responded philosophically: "Oh my! you can't really say; it's an it!" In younger years Mrs. Nevermore's heart possessed a native Roman paramour, Sor Carlo, and wherever you moved in Mrs. Nevermore's proximity, you could, at the end of a perspective of doorways, make out a seated Sor Carlo. Between Easter and October, you understand; for he was a wreck, and even now, outside the season, he was known to all the guests, but not openly acknowledged, as a ghost. He always sat motionlessly propped up against some wall or other, dressed in a filthy light-colored suit, his legs thick as columns from top to bottom, his proud face with his black-dyed Cavour beard distorted by fat and sadness. Only when I came home at night did I ever see him in motion. When all the eyes that otherwise stood guard over him were shut, then he dragged his gasping self through the corridors from bench to bench, and did battle with his faltering breath. He lived out his life here. I never failed to greet him, for which he thanked me with dignity. I don't know if he was grateful for Mrs. Nevermore's charity, or if out of protest against her ingratitude and because of his injured pride, he seemed to sleep all day with his eyes open. He also revealed nothing of what Mrs. Nevermore felt for her old Sor Carlo. One ought probably to assume that for her the tender equanimity of age long since outweighed the importance that young people place on such matters of the heart. On one occasion at least I found her with Sor Carlo in her office: Sor Carlo sat against one wall and directed his sleepy look through the opposite wall at infinity, and Mrs. Nevermore sat on her table and stared through the open door into the darkness. These two steady gazes, separated by approximately a yard's width, passed parallel to each other, and just beneath their periphery, beside the table legs, sat Michette, the cat, with the two house dogs. The blond Pomeranian Maik, with the soft balding hair and the onset of arthritis in the back, attempted to perform with Michette what dogs usually do with other dogs, and meanwhile, the fat, rusty-blond Pomeranian Ali goodnaturedly nibbled on her ear; nobody tried to stop this, neither Michette nor the two old people.

If anyone would have stopped it, it would certainly have

been Miss Frazer; though it is to be assumed that she would not have permitted Maik to start anything like that in her presence in the first place. Every evening Miss Frazer sat with us in the parlor on the edge of an easy chair; with her torso she leaned back straight as a board, so that it touched only the upper rim of the head rest. She stretched her legs out straight so that only her heels grazed the ground; in this position she crocheted. When she was finished, she sat herself down at the oval table in the midst of our conversation and did her daily lesson. This having been completed, with quick fingers she played two rounds of solitaire. And when the solitaire was over, she said good night and disappeared. It was then ten o'clock.

A deviation from the norm only occurred when one of us opened a window in the tropical heat of the parlor; then Miss Frazer stood up and shut it again. She probably couldn't stand the draft. We learned as little of the source of her aversion to the breeze as we knew of the contents of her daily lesson or the object of her handiwork. Miss Frazer was an old English spinstress; her profile was as knightly and sharp as that of a nobleman. On the other hand, her face, when viewed from the front, was round and red as an apple, with a sweet sprinkling of girlishness beneath her white hair. Whether she was also sweet-natured, no one knew. Except for the unavoidable civilities, she never exchanged a word with us. Perhaps she despised our idleness, our prattle, our immorality. Not even the Swiss gentleman, who for the last six hundred years had been a republican, did she grace with an intimate exhange. She knew everything about us, for she was always in our midst, and was the only person of whom we had no idea why she was there. All in all, with her crocheting, her lessons, and that red apple smile, she might well have been there for no other reason than for pleasure and to share our company.

Ill-Tempered Observations

Black Magic

1

Ever since the Russian variety show teams introduced them to us, these black hussars, these death's head grenadiers, these Arditi* seem to exist in every army on earth. They swore an oath of victory or death, and sport tailor-made black uniforms with white baldrics that look like the ribs of death; thus adorned, they parade around as they please to the everlasting delight of the ladies until they peacefully die—that is, as long as there is no war. They live by certain songs that have a somber accompaniment which lends them a dark radiance ideally suited for bedroom lighting.

As the curtain went up, seven such hussars sat around together on the little stage; it was rather dark and the bright snow outside shone through the windows. With their black uniforms and their painfully propped up heads they were scattered about in hypnotic formation in the dim light and accompanied a loudly singing comrade in a pitch-black luminous pianissimo. "Hear the horses pound the steppes

*Members of the elite Italian assault troops.

51

with their mighty hooves," they sang, all the way through
to the inevitable "if lady luck should run amuck, when the
swallows wander—."

2

An enigmatic soul suggests: if this were a painted picture,
then we would have a textbook example of kitsch. If it were
a "tableau vivant," we would have before us the unnerving
sentimentality of a once beloved parlor game, that is,
something half kitsch and half sad, like a glockenspiel that
has just been played. But since it is a singing tableau vivant,
what is it then? There is a certain sugary lustre to the trifles
performed by these splendid Russian emigrants, but one
only snickers in retrospect, whereas one would surely have
fumed before an oil painting of the same type: could it be
possible that kitsch grows ever more tolerable and ever less
kitschy if one, and then two, dimensions of kitsch are added
to it?

This hypothesis can neither be presumed nor denied.

But what happens if still another dimension of the same
is added, and it becomes reality? Have we not huddled in
bunkers, while some premonition of tomorrow hung in the
air and a comrade started singing? Oh, it felt so melan-
choly! And it was kitsch. But it was the sort of kitsch that
lay like another layer of sadness over our sadness, like an
unconfessed rancor at this forced camaraderie. There is so
much that one might have felt at this last eternal hour, and
the articulation of the fearful image of death is not
necessarily best rendered in oil.

Is not art then a tool we employ to peel the kitsch off life?
Layer by layer art strips life bare. The more abstract it gets,
the more transparent the air is. Can it be that the farther it
is removed from life, the clearer art becomes? What a backwards contention it is to claim that life is more important
than art! Life is good as long as it holds up to art: that in
life which cannot be employed for art's sake is kitsch!

But what is kitsch?

In a somewhat less propitious time, the poet X would have become a popular hack on a family magazine. He would then have presupposed that the heart always responds to certain situations with the same set feelings. Noble-mindedness would always have been recognizably noble, the abandoned child lamentable, and the summer landscape stirring. Notice that in this way, a firm, clearcut, and immutable relationship would have been established between the feelings and the words, true to the nature of the term kitsch. Thus kitsch, which prides itself so much on sentiment, turns sentiment into concepts.

As a function of the times, however, X, instead of being a good family magazine hack, has become a bad Expressionist. Consequently, his work causes intellectual short-circuiting. He appeals to Man, God, the Spirit, Goodness, Chaos; and out of such big words he squeezes his sophisticated sentences. He could not possibly do so, were he to imagine the totality of their meaning, or at least grasp their utter unimaginability. But long before his time, these words had already taken on connotations meaningful and meaningless, in books and newspapers; our Expressionist has often seen them wedged together, and the words need only be loaded with the least little bit of significance for him to perceive sparks flying between them. This, however, is only a consequence of the fact that he had not learned how to think based on the experience of his own imagination, but rather, with the aid of borrowed terms.

In both of the aforementioned instances, kitsch affirms itself as something that peels life off of language. Layer by layer, it strips language bare. The more abstract kitsch becomes, the more it becomes kitsch. The intellect is effective so long as it stands up to life.

But what is life?

Life is living: you cannot describe it to someone who does not know it. It is friendship and enmity, enthusiasm and disenchantment, peristalsis and ideology. Thinking has, among other functions, to establish an intellectual order in life. As well as to destroy that order. Every concept combines many disparate phenomena in life, and just as frequently, a single phenomenon will give rise to many new concepts. It is common knowledge that our poets have stopped wanting to think ever since they think they heard the philosophers say that thought is no longer supposed to be a matter of thinking, but rather of living.

Life is to blame for everything.

But in God's name: What is living?

5

Two syllogisms emerge from these assertions.

Art peels kitsch off of life.

Kitsch peels life off of language.

And: The more abstract art becomes, the more it becomes art.

Also: The more abstract kitsch becomes, the more it becomes kitsch.

These are two splendid syllogisms. If only we could resolve them!

According to the second, it appears that kitsch equals art. According to the first, however, kitsch equals language minus life. Art equals life minus kitsch equals life minus language plus life equals two lives minus language. But according to the second, life equals three times kitsch and, therefore, art equals six times kitsch minus language.

So what is art?

6

A black hussar has it so good. The black hussars swore an oath of victory or death and meanwhile stroll around in this uniform to the delight of all the ladies. That is not art! That's life!

But why then do we maintain that it's just a tableau vivant?

Doors and Portals

Doors are a thing of the past, even if back doors are still said to crop up at architectural competitions.

A door consists of a rectangular wooden frame set in the wall, on which a moveable board is fastened. This board at least is still barely comprehensible. For it is supposed to be light enough to be easily pivoted, and it fits in with the oak and walnut paneling that until recently adorned every proper living room. Yet even this board has already lost most of its significance. Up until the middle of the last century you could listen in with your ear pressed against it, and what secrets you could sometimes hear! The count had disowned his stepdaughter, and the hero, who was supposed to marry her, heard just in time that they planned to poison him. Let anybody try such a feat in a contemporary house! Before he even got to listen in at the door, he'd have long since heard everything through the walls. And what's more: not even the faintest thought would have escaped his ear. Why has no radio-poet yet taken advantage of the possibilities of the modern concrete structure?! It is undoubtedly the predestined stage for the radio play!

Still far more outdated than the door itself is the doorframe. If you cast a glance past open doors, through a suite of rooms, you'd think you were experiencing the nightmare vision of a soccer forward faced by an infinite succession of goal posts. There is also a kind of gallows of which it reminds us. Why do they do it this way? Technically, a snug closure could be achieved without these doorposts; in fact, they are only there to please the eye. It is assumed that the eye would find it too bare if the door were fastened to the wall or to an invisible metal band. To the studied eye this would be no different than the absence of a cuff peering forth between the hand and the arm. Indeed, these door frames have a similar history to that of the detachable cuffs. When rooms were still vaulted, such a feature was unknown; the door turned on two lovely cast iron hinges. Later they learned to build flat roofs that were supported by heavy wooden beams; proud of this innovation, they left the beams visible and likewise covered the spaces between them with wood, and the result was those beautiful wainscotted ceilings. Later still, they covered the beams beneath a stuccoed ceiling, but around the doors a narrow wooden rim was preserved.

And finally, today, they build walls of reinforced concrete instead of brick. But the narrow wooden rim, lonesome, senseless, that seems to come out of nowhere and is related only to the window frame, is left as a remnant of the custom. Isn't that exactly the same as the history of the shirt, which first began as a wide, visible garment with neck and hand frills? Later it disappeared beneath the frock coat, but collar and cuff still peaked forth beneath the neck and sleeves of the suit. Then the collar and cuff were separated from the shirt, and finally, prior to any further improvement, the removable collar and cuff became solitary symbols of culture, which, in order to demonstrate proper manners, were buttoned onto a hidden undergarment.

This discovery—that wooden doors are removable cuffs— must be credited to the famous architect who realized that since man is born in a clinic and dies in a hospital, he likewise requires asceptic restraint in the design of his living space. We call this sort of phenomenon a spontaneous architectural development born out of the spirit of the times; but evidently things are a little difficult nowadays. The man of former times, whether lord of the manor or citydweller, lived in his house; his station in life manifested itself therein, had accumulated there. In the Biedermeier period you still held open house; today we merely imitate the custom. Back then your house served the purpose of maintaining appearances for which there is always money at hand; today, however, there are other objects that satisfy this same purpose: travel, cars, sports, winter vacations, suites in luxury hotels. Nowadays, the fantasy of showing what you are is lived out in this way, and if a rich man nevertheless builds himself a house, there is something artificial, something private in the act, which is no longer the fulfillment of a universal wish. And how then should there be doors if there is no "house"?! The only original door conceived by our time is the glass revolving door of the hotel and the department store.

In former times, the door, as a part of the whole, represented the entire house, just as the house one owned and the house which one was having built were intended to show the social standing of its owner. The door was an entrance into a society of privilege, which was opened or shut in the face of the new arrival, depending on who he was; generally it decided his fate. However, it was likewise perfectly well suited to the little man who didn't count for much outside, but who behind his door could immediately play god. For this reason, the door was cherished by all and fulfilled a living purpose in the popular imagination. The noble folk could open or shut their doors, and the burgher could moreover keep knocking when the door is already open. He could also force it open. He could transact his business in the doorway, as it were. He could turn away from his own or a stranger's door. He could shut the door in someone's face, could show him to the door; indeed, he could even throw him out the door: this was an abundance of relations with respect to life, and they demonstrate that excellent mixture of realism and symbolism that language achieves when something is very important to us.

The great age of doors is behind us! It may be very spectacular to call out to someone that you are going to throw them out the door, but who has ever really seen someone "flying" out? Even if it is sometimes attempted, the procedure seldom still has that one-sided quality which constitutes its charm, for the required competence and strength is sadly lacking nowadays. We don't even slam the door in anyone's face anymore, but rather refuse to receive the telephoned announcement of an unwanted visit in advance; and to sweep in front of one's door—that is, to mind one's own business—has become an inconceivable suggestion. These have long since become unreasonable figures of speech and are nothing now but sweet illusions that creep up on us with a sentimental longing every time we look at an old-fashioned portal. It is the fading history surrounding a hole that, for the time being, has still been left open to the carpenter.

Monuments

Aside from the fact that you never know whether to refer to them as monuments or memorials, monuments do have all kinds of other characteristics. The most salient of these is a bit contradictory; namely, that monuments are so conspicuously inconspicuous. There is nothing in this world as invisible as a monument. They are no doubt erected to be seen—indeed, to attract attention. But at the same time they are impregnated with something that repels attention, causing the glance to roll right off, like water droplets off an oilcloth, without even pausing for a moment. You can walk down the same street for months, know every address, every show window, every policeman along the way, and you won't even miss a dime that some-one dropped on the sidewalk; but you are very surprised when one day, staring up at a pretty chambermaid on the first floor of a building, you notice a not-at-all-tiny metal plaque on which, engraved in indelible letters, you read that from eighteen hundred and such and such to eighteen hundred and a little more the unforgettable So-and-so lived and created here.

Many people have this same experience even with larger-than-life-sized statues. Every day you have to walk around them, or use their pedestal as a haven of rest, you employ them as a compass or a distance marker; when you happen upon the well-known square, you sense them as you would a tree, as part of the street scenery, and you would be momentarily stunned were they to be missing one morning: but you never look at them, and do not generally have the slightest notion of whom they are supposed to represent, except that maybe you know if it's a man or a woman.

It would be wrong to let ourselves be deceived by certain exceptions to the rule. As, for instance, those few statues which, Baedecker in hand, we seek out, like the Gattamelata or the Colleoni, this being a very particular example; or memorial towers that block off an entire landscape; or monuments that form a series, like the Bismarck monuments scattered all over Germany.

Such forceful monuments do exist; and then there are also those that embody the expression of a living thought or feeling: it is, however, the purpose of most ordinary monuments to first conjure up a remembrance, or to grab hold of our attention and give a pious bent to our feelings, for this, it is assumed, is what we more or less need; and it is in this, their prime purpose, that monuments always fall short. They repel the very thing they are supposed to attract. One cannot say we did not notice them; one would have to say they "de-notice" us, they elude our perceptive faculties: this is a downright vandalism-inciting quality of theirs!

This can no doubt be explained. Anything that endures over time sacrifices its ability to make an impression. Anything that constitutes the walls of our life, the backdrop of our consciousness, so to speak, forfeits its capacity to play a role in that consciousness. A constant, bothersome sound becomes inaudible after several hours. Pictures that we hang up on the wall are in a matter of days soaked up by the wall; only very rarely do we stand before them and look at them. Half-read books once replaced among the splendid rows of books in our library will never be read to the end. Indeed, it is enough for some sensitive souls to buy a book whose beginning they like, and then never pick it up again.

In this case, the attitude is already becoming outright aggressive; one can, however, also follow its inexorable course in the realm of feelings, in which case it is always aggressive, in family life, for instance. Here the firm bond of marriage is distinguished from the fickleness of desire by the much repeated sentence: Do I have to tell you every fifteen minutes that I love you?! And to what heightened degree must these psychological detriments of durability manifest themselves in bronze and marble!

If we mean well by monuments, we must inevitably come to the conclusion that they make demands on us that run contrary to our nature, and for the fulfillment of which very particular preparations are required. It would be a crime to want to make the danger signs for cars as inconspicuously monochrome as monuments. Locomotives, after all, blow shrill, not sleepy tones, and even mailboxes are accorded alluring colors. In short, monuments ought also to try a little harder, as we must all do nowadays! It is easy for them to stand around quietly, accepting occasional glances; we have a right to ask more of our monuments today. Once we have grasped this idea—which, thanks to certain current conceptual tendencies, is slowly making inroads—we recognize how backward our monument art is in comparison to contemporary developments in advertising. Why doesn't our bronze-cast hero at least resort to the gimmick, long since outdated elsewhere, of tapping with his finger on a pane of glass? Why don't the figures in a marble group turn, like those better-made figures in show windows do, or at least blink their eyes open and shut? The very minimum that we ought to ask of monuments, to make them attract attention, would be tried and true logos, like "Goethe's Faust is the best!" or "The dramatic ideas of the famous poet X are the cheapest!"

Unfortunately, the sculptors won't have any of this. They do not, so it seems, comprehend our age of noise and movement. If they represent a man in civilian clothes, he sits motionlessly in a chair or stands there, his hand stuck in between the second and third button of his jacket.

Sometimes he also holds a scroll in his hand, and no expression flutters across his face. He generally looks like one of the acute melancholics in the mental hospitals. If people were not oblivious to monuments and could observe what was going on up there, they'd shudder when passing, as you do beside the walls of a madhouse. It is even more frightening when the sculptors depict a general or a prince. His flag is waving in his hand, and there's no wind. His sword is drawn and no one draws back in fear. His arm motions imperiously forwards, and no man would think of following him. Even his horse, rearing, with sprayed nostrils, ready to jump, remains balanced on its hindlegs, astonished that the people down below, instead of stepping aside, quietly stuff a sandwich into their mouths or buy a paper. By God, the figures in monuments never make a move and yet remain forever frozen in a faux pas. It is a desperate situation.

I believe that I have in these remarks contributed a little something to the understanding of monument figures, memorial plaques, and the like. Maybe someone or other will henceforth look at them on his way home. But what I find ever more incomprehensible, the more I think about it, is the question, Why then, matters being the way they are, are monuments erected precisely for great men? This seems to be a carefully calculated insult. Since we can do them no more harm in life, we thrust them with a memorial stone hung around their neck into the sea of oblivion.

The Paintspreader

If over the course of the years you are compelled to pass through painting exhibitions, then surely one day you are bound to invent the term paintspreader. He is to the painter what the penpusher is to the poet. The term gives order to a hodgepodge of disparate phenomena. Since the beginning of our reckoning of time penpushers have lived off adaptations of the ten commandments and a few fables handed down to them by antiquity; the assumption that paintspreading is likewise based on a few fundamental principles is not therefore altogether out of the question.

Ten such principles would not be too few. For if you apply ten artistic principles effectively, that is, combined in alternating order, the result, mistakes in calculation notwithstanding, is three million, six-hundred twenty-eight thousand, and eight hundred different combinations. Each of these combinations would be different from the others, and all of them nonetheless still the same. The connoisseur could spend his life counting: one-two-three-four-five . . . , two-one-three-four-five . . . , three-two-one-four-five . . . and so on. Naturally the connoisseur would be indignant and would perceive this as a threat to his accomplished abilities.

It also seems that after several hundred thousand paint-spreaders the whole business would become ridiculous, and they would then switch artistic "directions." You can see what an artistic direction is, the moment you set foot in an exhibition hall. You would be more hard-pressed to recognize it, if you had to pass before a single solitary painting; but spread over many walls, artistic schools, directions, and periods are as easily distinguishable, one from another, as wallpaper patterns. On the other hand, the theoretical underpinnings of these various schools, directions, and periods usually remain unclear. This is by no means meant as a slight upon the paintspreaders; they produce honest work, are well-versed in their craft and are personally, for the most part, distinctive fellows. But the production statistics level out all differences.

We do however have to acknowledge one disadvantage that works against them: the fact that their paintings hang openly on the wall. Books have the advantage of being bound, and often uncut. They therefore stay famous longer; they maintain their freshness, and fame, after all, begins at that point at which you have heard of something but are not familiar with it. The paintspreaders, on the other hand, have the advantage of being more regularly sought out and "written up" than are the penpushers. If it weren't for the art market, how difficult it would be to decide which work you prefer! Christ, in his day, drove the dealers out of the Temple: I, however, am convinced that if you possess the true faith, you must also be able to sell it; then you could also adorn yourself with it, and then there would be a great deal more faith in the world than there is now!

Another advantage enjoyed by painting is that there is a method to it. Anyone can write. Perhaps everyone can paint too, but this fact is less well-known. Techniques and styles were invented to envelop painting in a shroud of mystery. Not everyone can paint like someone else; to do that, you have to first learn how. Those elementary school children

66

so rightfully admired nowadays for their painting talents would flunk out in any art academy; but the academic painter must likewise take great pains to unlearn his acquired technique in order to drop his conventions and draw like a child. It is, all in all, a historic error to believe that the master makes the school; the students make it!

If we examine the matter more closely, however, it is not true either that anyone can write; quite the contrary, nobody can—everyone can merely take dictation and copy. It is impossible that a poem of Goethe's could come into being today; and even if by some miracle, Goethe were to write it himself, it would still be an anachronistic and in many ways dubious new poem, even though a splendid masterpiece of old! Is there any other explanation for this mystery than that this poem would not seem as though it had been copied from any contemporary poem, except perhaps for those poems that were themselves copied from it? Contemporaneity always means copying. Our ancestors wrote prose in long, beautiful sentences, convoluted like curls; although we still learn to do it that way in school, we write in short sentences that cut more quickly to the heart of the matter; and no one in the world can free his thinking from the manner in which his time wears the cloak of language. Thus no man can know to what extent he actually means what he writes and in writing, it is far less that people twist words than it is that words twist people.

Is it possible then too that not everyone can paint after all? Clearly, the painter cannot, not in the sense that the paintspreader associates with the word. The painter and the poet are above all, in the eyes of their contemporaries, those who cannot do what the paintspreaders and the penpushers can do. This is why so many penpushers consider themselves poets and so many paintspreaders painters. The difference usually only becomes apparent once it's too late. For by that time, a new generation of pushers and spreaders have come of age who already know what the painter and poet have only just learned.

This also explains why the painter and the poet always appear to belong to the past or the future; they are forever being awaited or declared extinct. If, however, on occasion one actually happens to pass for the real thing, it isn't always necessarily the right one.

A Culture Question

Can you tell us what a poet is?

This question ought some time to appear in one of those intellectual competitions in which people dispute the issue: "Who murdered Mr. Stein? (in the novel whose serialization begins in tomorrow's Sunday supplement)" Or: "What should Roman-three do, if Roman-one makes a different play from the one suggested in the last bridge congress?"

It is not however to be expected that a newspaper would readily follow this suggestion, and if it did, then the editors would phrase the question in a more engaging manner. Like this, for instance: "Who is your favorite poet?" But also like this: "Who in your opinion is the greatest contemporary poet?" and "What was the best book of the year?" (also: "of the month?"). Such questions seem to suggest themselves because of their stimulating effect.

In this way, people learn from time to time what kinds of poets there are, and there are always the greatest, the most important, the most genuine, the most recognized, and the most read. But what, without a superlative, the poet is, and when someone who simply writes is a poet, and not the "well-known author of . . . ,"—this question has been raised since time immemorial. The issue is clear, and yet the world is ashamed of asking such a question, as though it smacked of the archaic! Yet it will surely come to pass that you will be able to say with certainty what *Kaffee Hag*, a Rolls Royce, and what a glider are, but will be at a loss, when your children's children ask eagerly: "Great-grandpa, in your day you still had poets, what's that?"

Perhaps you will try to convince them that poets were about as real as Hell. For we still say with the greatest conviction: "Aw, hell!" "Go to hell!" "Hell's bells!" "Come hell or high water!" and the like, without really believing in Hell. It's just a question of the life of a language, and no insurance company would put the smallest premium on the life of the German language. But this argument can easily be rebutted. For however insignificant a role the word "poet" may play in the intellectual history of our time, future generations will find its unexpected, albeit inextinguishable, traces in our economic history! Consider how many people nowadays live off the word poet—the number is almost infinite, even if we completely ignore the wondrous lie claimed by the state, that its executive purpose is the cultivation of the arts and sciences. We might begin by counting the literary professorships and seminars, and proceed to include the entire university structure with its bursars, proctors, secretaries, and others involved in its administration. Or else we can begin with the publishers, and then move on to the publishing concerns with their employees, the agents, the retail booksellers, the printers, the paper and press manufacturers, the trains, the post office, the tax collection office, the newspapers, the ministerial department heads, the superintendants—in short, with enough patience, anyone could spend an entire day calculating the web of these connections. What will always remain a constant is the fact that all of these thousands of people live—some well, some badly, some completely, some in part—off the existence of poets: Although no one knows what a poet is, no one can say for certain that he has ever seen a poet, and all of the prize competitions, academies, honors, honoraria, and distributions of honored titles cannot give any assurance that you can find a living example.

I would estimate that in the whole world today no more than a few dozen of them are still to be found. It is uncertain whether they can live off the fact that we live off of them: some will succeed at this, others will not—it is an open-ended issue. If we wanted to cite a similar situation for comparison's sake, we might say that countless people live off the fact that there are chickens, or that there are fish; yet the fish and chickens do not live from this, but rather die from it. In fact, we might add that even our chickens and fish live for a short while off the fact that they must die. But this entire comparison proves untenable when we consider that at least we know what these creatures are, that they actually exist and that they constitute no disruption to the fish and chicken breeding industry, whereas the poet, quite the contrary, constitutes a definite disturbance to the businesses built up around his handiwork. If he has money or luck, no one will bother too much over him; but as soon as he makes so bold, lacking the two aforementioned commodities, as to claim his birthright, wherever he happens to come from, he necessarily resembles a ghost who has the gall to remind us of a loan granted to our forefathers at the time of the ancient Greeks.

After a few trivial idealistic protestations by the publishers, he would be asked whether he believed he could produce a piece of literature that could guarantee a minimum sales run of thirty thousand copies; and the editors would recommend that he write short stories, which, however, would have to conform, as is only natural, to the needs of a newspaper. He however would necessarily reply that he could not consent to such terms; and he could likewise expect to arouse an equally legitimate displeasure at stage guilds, literary councils, and other cultural organizations. For everyone means well by him, and considering the fact that he can neither write popular plays, best-selling novels nor movies, we are inclined to come to the dark conclusion that if we were to add up all the things that this man cannot do, all that might perhaps be left over would be the fact that he possesses an uncommon talent. This being the case, we cannot help him either, and we would have to be inhuman not to hold it against him, not to want to be free of him.

When on one occasion such a needy ghost scoured the Berlin literary depots, an adroit, young, smartly dressed penpusher who had mastered the most out-of-the-way means of making a living, and for that reason believed that he too had been through the treadmill, expressed this by bursting forth with the following impassioned statement: "My God, if I had as much talent as this jackass, what couldn't I accomplish!" He was mistaken.

Surrounded by Poets and Thinkers

They say that books have no magnitude nowadays and that writers are no longer able to write lengthy works. This may undoubtedly be so; but, for once, why not look at it the other way around, and consider the possibility that the German reader no longer knows how to read? Does not the reader develop in ever greater measure, the longer the text, an as yet unexplained resistance (not to be confused with displeasure), particularly if the text is genuinely poetic? It is as though the portal through which the book must pass were pathologically chafed and had shut itself up tight. When faced with the task of reading a book, many people nowadays find themselves thrust into an unnatural frame of mind; they feel as though they were made to undergo a disagreeable operation in which they have no confidence.

If we search for the reason and listen in on conversations on the subject, we find that the reader—the good reader, who would not miss a single important book, and who is quick to name the geniuses of the day and the age!—we find that even this reader will almost always faithlessly concede, as soon as he is confronted with strong opposition to his opinion, that in all seriousness his favored genius may in fact not be a genius at all, and that there are no real geniuses around these days. This discovery however is by no means restricted to belles-lettres. Medicine has faltered, mathematics is up in the clouds, philosophy has lost its sense of purpose: everywhere you turn today, the layman has lost his respect for the expert. And since every expert is also a layman in hundreds of other fields, the result is a great profusion of serious misgivings.

It is of course difficult to say just exactly how great today's poets, thinkers, and scientists really are; but that has nothing whatsoever to do with the subject of our deliberations, for, as we readily discover, this phenomenon resembles in its structure the well-known children's card game, "Old Maid." The poets do not after all find fault in themselves, but rather in the scientists, thinkers, technicians, and other luminaries; and the same is true for the others. In short, the bulk of this cultural pessimism that seems to oppress everyone is always shifted onto someone else's shoulders; and plainly put, man as culture-consumer is, in an insidious way, dissatisfied with man as culture-producer. This claim, however, accords wonderfully well with its opposite; for just as often as you hear the complaint that true genius no longer exists, so you too might be inclined to remark in private that there is nothing but genius left. Just take a moment to leaf through the news and reviews in our magazines and newspapers, and you will truly be amazed at how many deeply moving, prophetic, greatest, deepest, and very great masters appear over the course of a few months; and how often in the span of such a brief period, "finally another true poet" has been granted to the nation; and how often the most beautiful animal story and the best novel of the last ten years is written. A few weeks later hardly anyone can still remember the unforgettable impression they made.

Here we may add the second observation, that all such judgements derive from diverse circles hermetically closed off to each other. They are formed by related publishers, authors, critics, newspapers, readers, and miscellaneous successes, each of whom does not have contact with anyone outside his particular circle; and all of these large and small circles, whose cohesiveness may well be compared to that of a romantic entanglement or a political party, have their own geniuses or at least their "No-one-else more worthy of the title." True, a circle is formed of the most successful people from different circles, but we should not be deceived by this; it would appear as if the truly significant would not after all go unnoticed, and that a nation were eagerly waiting to take such significance in, but in reality, the all-around success is the progeny of a rather discordant set of parents; for what is admired is not so much that which has something to say to everyone, but rather that which leaves each his own. And just as fame is a mixed bag, so too are the famous a motley crew.

If we do not limit ourselves to the realm of belle-lettres, their image as a group is overwhelming. For the circle, the ring of people, the school, or the widespread success that emanates from anyone involved in an intellectual activity is negligible compared to the plenitude of sects whose souls are nourished on eating cherries, on the theater of the great outdoors, on musical gymnastics, on Eubiotics, or any one of a thousand other oddities. It is impossible to say how many such Romes there are, each of which has its own Pope, whose name the uninitiated have never heard, whose followers, however, look to him for the salvation of mankind. All of Germany is teeming with such spiritual brotherhoods: and from this great Germany, in which famous scientists can only live by their teaching and select poets at best by marketing journalistic bagatelles, from this same Germany, innumerable lunatics are swarmed with the means and the participants for the development of their whims, for the printing of their books and for the founding of their periodicals. For that reason, before bad times recently set in in Germany, more than a thousand magazines were founded annually and more than thirty thousand books appeared, and this was deemed the sign of a towering intellectual achievement.

It is unfortunately to be assumed with infinitely greater certainty that this will rather turn out to have been a sign, not recognized early enough, of the spread of a dangerous group-mania. Infected by this mania, thousands of little groups each peddle their own set notion of life, so that it ought not to surprise us if soon a genuine paranoiac will hardly still be able to resist competing with the amateurs.

Art Anniversary

> "It is easier to predict what the world will be doing a hundred years from now than to predict how it will write in a hundred years. Why? The entire answer isn't fit for a dinner table conversation." (From an unfinished book that will offer a more serious answer to the question [cf. *Diaries* . . . pp. 578 and 850]).

If, as is the case from time to time, you happen to re-encounter a play or a novel which twenty years ago grabbed hold of your soul, along with the souls of many others, you experience something which has actually never been explained, since apparently everyone takes it for granted: the sparkle is gone, the importance has disappeared, dust and moths fly off at your touch. But why this aging must take place, and what exactly is altered in the process, this no one knows. The comedy of all art anniversaries consists of the old admirers making solemn, uneasy faces, as if their collar button had slipped down behind their shirt front.

It is not the same as re-encountering a flame of your youth who has not grown any prettier over the years. For in the latter case you no longer even comprehend what once made you stutter, although at least it has something to do with the touching transitory nature of all earthly pursuits and the notoriously fickle nature of love. But a work of literature that you re-encounter is like an old sweetheart who for twenty years has been embalmed in alcohol: not a hair is different, and not a fleck of her rosy epidermis has changed. A shiver rolls down your spine! Now you are supposed to be once again who you were: one semblance demands another. It is a stretching torture, in the course of which the soles have remained in place, but the rest of the body has been twisted a thousand times around the revolving world!

Reliving a former art experience is also different from meeting the other ghosts of old arousals and infatuations: enemies, friends, wild nights, passions endured and surmounted. All this and the conditions that surrounded it sink into oblivion as soon as the fling is over: it has fulfilled some purpose and was absorbed by the fulfillment; it was a denial in one's life or a stage in the development of your personality. But bygone art served nothing; its former effect has disappeared unnoticed, lost itself along the way; it is a stage for no one. For do you really feel yourself to be standing on a higher plateau when looking down upon a once admired work? You stand no higher, just elsewhere! Indeed, to tell the truth, even if, while standing before an old painting, you realize with a comfortable, hardly suppressed yawn that you no longer need be enthusiastic about it, you are still far from being enthused by the fact that there are new paintings to be admired. You simply feel yourself to have slipped from one timely compulsion to another, which by no means excludes the fact that you went about it perfectly voluntarily and actively; voluntary and involuntary behavior are not after all direct opposites, they also blend in equal parts, so that ultimately, you involuntarily overindulge in voluntary behavior, or voluntarily the involuntary, as is often the case in life.

Still, in this elsewhere you will find a remarkable dose of transcendence. It is, we realize, if appearances do not deceive, related to fashion. Fashion, after all, is not only marked by the one characteristic, namely, that you find it ridiculous in retrospect, but also by the other, that as long as *a* fashion lasts, you can hardly imagine taking seriously the opinions of a man who is not dressed from head to toe just as ridiculously as you yourself are. I would not know what in our admiration of antiquity could shield a budding philospher from suicide, if not the fact that Plato and Aristotle wore no pants; pants have contributed far more than you might think to the intellectual development of Europe, for without them, Europeans would most likely never have gotten over their classical-humanistic inferiority complex vis-à-vis the antique. Thus we hold our time's most profound feeling—that we would not barter with anyone who wasn't dressed in contemporary clothing. And even of art we only feel for that same reason a sense of progress with each new year; although it may simply be a coincidence that art exhibits, like the latest fashion, appear in the spring and fall. This sense of progress is not pleasant. It reminds you, in the most extreme way, of a dream in which you are seated on a horse and cannot get off, because the horse never stands still. You would gladly take pleasure in progress, if only it took a pause. If only we could stop for a moment on our high horse, look back, and say to the past: look where I am now! But already the uncanny process continues, and after experiencing it several times, you begin to feel queasy in the stomach with those four strange legs trotting beneath you, constantly carrying you forward.

But what conclusions may we draw from the fact that it is just as ridiculously unpleasant to look at old fashions (so long as they have not yet become costumes), as it is ridiculously unpleasant to look at old pictures, or the outmoded facades of old-style houses, and to read yesterday's books? Clearly, there is no other conclusion except that we become unpleasant to ourselves the moment we gain some distance from what we were. This stretch of self-loathing begins several years before now and ends approximately with our grandparents, that is, the time to which we begin to be indifferent. It is only then that what was is no longer outdated, but begins to be old; it is our past, and no longer that which passed away from us. But what we ourselves did and were lies almost completely in the realm of self-loathing. It would indeed be intolerable to be reminded of everything that we once considered most important, and the great majority of people would remain surprisingly little moved if, at an advanced age, you were to show them again, in the form of a movie, their grandest gestures and once most stirring scenes.

How are we to make sense of this? Apparently inherent to the nature of temporal matters is a certain degree of exaggeration, a "superplus" and superabundance. Even a slap in the face requires more rage than you can be accountable for. This enthusiasm of "now" burns up, and as soon as it has become superfluous, it is extinguished by forgetting, a very productive and fertile activity by means of which we only really first become—and are ever and anew reconstituted as—that easygoing, pleasant, and consequent person for whose sake we excuse everything on earth.

Art rocks the boat in this regard. Nothing emanates from it that could endure without enthusiasm. It is, as it were, nothing but enthusiasm without bones and ashes, pure enthusiasm that burns for no reason and nonetheless is stuck in a frame or in between the covers of a book, as though nothing had happened. It never becomes our past, but always remains that which has passed from us. It is understandable then that we should look back at it every ten or twenty-five years with an uneasy eye!

Only great art, that indeed which alone, strictly speaking, merits being called art, constitutes an exception. But the latter has never really fit that well in the society of the living.

80

Binoculars

Slow motion pictures dive beneath the agitated surface, and it is their magic that permits the spectator to see himself with open eyes, as it were, swimming among the objects of life. Movies may have popularized this phenomenon; but it has long been available to us by a means still to be recommended nowadays because of its convenience: by looking, that is, through a telescope at objects that one would usually not watch through a telescope. An experiment of this sort is described in the following pages.

The first object of our attention was a sign on the gate of a beautiful old building located directly opposite our observation post, a building that houses a well-known government agency. This sign proclaimed, through the binocular lens, that the government agency held office hours from nine to four. This already elicited the observer's surprise; for it was three o'clock, and not only was there no official in sight, but the observer could not recall ever having seen with his naked eye an official in the agency at this hour. Finally he discovered two tiny figures standing close together behind a remote window, drumming with their fingers on the windowpane and staring down at the street. And no sooner had he discovered them, than, as they stood there trapped in the little circle of his instrument, he understood with warm sympathy and realized with pride how important this telescoping function might yet become for bureaucrats, and for men in general who have a sacrosanct number of hours to sit out in an office.

The second object of his attention was the building itself. It was an old palace with a festoon of fruit on the capital of the stone pillars and a beautiful articulation of the facade in height and breadth, and while the spyglass still searched for the officials in attendance, the observer was already struck by how clearly this support structure, these windows and cornices had positioned themselves in the circle of his looking glass; now that he had taken it all in with a single glance, he was almost startled at the stony perspectival exactitude with which it all returned his gaze. He suddenly realized that these horizontal lines that conjoined at some point toward the back of the building, these contracting windows that became all the more trapezoid the farther to the side they were situated—indeed, this entire avalanche of reasonable, familiar limitations into a funnel of foreshortening located somewhere to the side and to the rear—that all this had until now struck him as a Renaissance nightmare: an awful painter's legend, actually, of disappearing lines, reputedly exaggerated, though there may also be some truth to it. But now he saw it before his very eyes, magnified to more than life-size, and looking far worse than the most unlikely rumor.

And if you don't believe that the world is really like this, just focus on a streetcar. The trolley made an S-shaped double curve in front of the palace. Countless times from his second story window, the observer had witnessed it approaching, seen it make this very S-shaped double curve and drive away again: at every stage of this development, the same elongated red train. But when he watched it through the binoculars, he noticed something completely different: an inexplicable force suddenly pressed this contraption together like a cardboard box, its walls squeezed ever more obliquely together (any minute it would be completely flat); then the force let up, the car grew wide to the rear, a movement swept once again over all its surfaces, and while the flabbergasted eyewitness released the breath he had held in his breast, the trusty old red box was back to its normal shape again. All this happened so clearly, so out in the open, as he watched it with his lens (and not just in the private chamber of his eye), that he could have sworn it was no less real than watching a fan being opened and shut. And if you don't believe it, you can try it yourself. All you need is an apartment toward which a streetcar approaches in an S-shaped curve.

Once this discovery had been made, the discoverer naturally turned to watching women; and thus was revealed to him the whole inescapable significance of human architectonics. That which in a woman is round, and according to the fashion of the day was then more painstakingly hidden than it is today (so that it looked like nothing more than a small rythmic irregularity in the otherwise boyish flow of motion), arched inwards again, under the incorruptible eye of the binoculars, turning back into those ancient simple hills that constitute the eternal landscape of love. And round about, unexpectedly, a myriad of whispering folds, aroused by every step, opened and shut in her dress. They announced to the naked eye the inviolable appearance of the wearer or the talents of the tailor, and secretly revealed that which is not shown; for when magnified, impulses are actualized, and when viewed through the tube of the looking glass, every woman becomes a psychologically spied Susannah in the bath of her dress. But it was amazing how soon such a sophisticated curiosity evaporated under the immovable and clearly somewhat spiteful equanimity of the binoculars' glance; and nothing remained but the trifling and flicker of those eternally constant values that require no psychology.

Enough of this! The best way to insure against an obscene misuse of this philosophical tool is to ponder its theory, "Isolation." We always see things amidst their surroundings and generally perceive them according to what function they serve in that context. But remove them from that context and they suddenly become incomprehensible and terrible, the way things must have been on the first day after creation, before the new phenomena had yet grown accustomed to each other and to us. So too, in the luminous solitude of our telescopic circle, everything becomes clearer and larger, but above all, things become more arcane and demonic. A hat which, according to common custom crowns the masculine figure and is synonymous with the overall appearance of the man of worldly influence and power (an altogether skittish form, belonging to the body as well as the soul), instantly degenerates into something insane when the binoculars strip it of its romantic attachments to the world around it and restore its true isolated optical presence. A woman's charm is fatally undercut as soon as the lens perceives her from the hem of her skirt upwards as a sack-like space from which two twisted little stilts peer forth. And how frightening does the ivory flashing of love become, and how infantilely comical is anger, when both are separated from their effect, isolated in the circle of the lens! There is between our clothes and ourselves, and between our customs and ourselves, a convoluted relationship of moral credit according to which we first lend customs and clothes their entire significance, and then borrow it back again, paying interest on the interest; and this is why we border on bankruptcy when we cut off their line of credit.

Naturally this has some bearing on the much ridiculed absurdities of fashion, which one year make us longer and shorten us the next, which make us first fat and then skinny, sometimes wide on top and narrow on the bottom, sometimes narrow on top and wide down below, which one year prescribe that everything be combed upwards, and the next year insist that everything be combed back downwards again, impelling us now to brush our hair forwards and backwards, now to the right and to the left. If we consider it all from a wholly unsympathetic standpoint, fashion offers us an astoundingly limited number of geometric possibilities, among which we alternate in the most passionate way, without ever totally disrupting the tradition. If we likewise include the fashions of thought, feeling, and action, about which practically the same can be said, then our entire history must appear to the sensitized eye as nothing but a corral, within the confines of which the human hoard stampedes senselessly back and forth. And yet how willingly we follow the leaders, who themselves merely charge ahead of us out of terror, and what joy grins back at us in the mirror when we connect with the fashionable norm, looking exactly like everyone else, even though everyone looks different than they did yesterday! Why do we need all this?! Perhaps we fear, and rightfully so, that our character would scatter like a powder if we did not pack it into a publicly approved container.

The observer ended finally at foot level, that is, at that point where man raised himself upright out of the animal domain. And how uncanny is that spot in the case of the communion between man and woman! We do after all have some prior knowledge of this sphere from the movies, in which famous heroes and heroines waddle rapidly toward us like ducks. But the cinema serves our love of life, and makes every effort to beautify its deficiencies, at which purpose it succeeds with ever greater technical proficiency. Not so our binoculars! They persist unrelentingly in showing us how ridiculously the legs disengage themselves from the hips and how clumsily they land on the heel and sole; not only does this organ swing inhumanly and land fat end first, but it likewise manages meanwhile to effect the most revealing personal grimaces.

The man with his eye to the instrument noticed two such instances in the course of five minutes. Hardly had he aimed at a young fellow decked out in a sportscap (whose socks were striped like the neck of a ring dove), when he likewise noticed how with a concentrated and tiny jerk in each of his slow steps, this fellow knocked the leg of the girl sauntering beside him out of sync. No doctor, no girl, not even he himself had any inkling of the awful prospects that lay ahead; only the binoculars detached this tiny gesture of helplessness from the universal harmony of brutality and allowed the approaching future to appear in the site! Something more harmless happened to the plump and friendly man in his prime who came quickly walking by and offered the world a kindly, obliging stride: according to a line down the middle of the site that neatly severed the legs one from another, it became apparent that his feet were repulsively twisted inwards; and now that at this one spot the curtain of truth had been lifted, one could see that his arms also swung selfishly in their shoulder sockets, that his shoulders tugged on the nape of his neck, and instead of revealing a benevolent overall appearance, all at once revealed a human system solely concerned with itself, a personality that couldn't give a hoot about anyone else!

In this way, the binoculars contribute both to our understanding of the individual, as well as to an ever deepening lack of comprehension of the nature of humanity. By dissolving the commonplace connections and discovering new ones, it in fact replaces the practice of genius, or is at least a preliminary exercise. And yet perhaps for this very reason we recommend this instrument in vain. Do not people, after all, employ it even at the theater to heighten the illusion, or during intermission, to see who else is there, thereby seeking not the unfamiliar, but rather, the comforting aspect of familiar faces?

It's Lovely Here

There are many people who on their vacations are drawn
to famous places. They drink beer in their hotel gardens,
and if in addition they happen to make pleasant acquain-
tances, they already look forward to the memories. On the
last day of their vacation they go to the nearest stationers;
they buy picture postcards there, and then buy more
postcards from the waiter back at the hotel. The picture
postcards that these people buy look the same all over the
world. They are tinted: the trees and lawns, poison green;
the sky, peacock blue; the cliffs are grey and red. The houses
are presented in downright painful relief, as though at any
moment they might spring up out of the surface; and the
color is so intense that a narrow band of it generally forms
a contour on the flip side of the card. If the world really
looked like that, one could indeed do nothing better than
affix a stamp to it and toss it in the nearest mailbox. On
these picture postcards people write: "It is indescribably
beautiful here." Or "It's lovely here." Or: "Too bad you
couldn't be here with me to see all this beauty." Sometimes
they also write: "You have no idea how beautiful it is here."
Or: "What a swell time we're having here!"

You really do have to understand these people correctly!

87

They are very happy indeed to be on a vacation trip and to see so many beautiful things that others cannot see; but it causes them pain and embarrassment actually to have to look at these things. If a tower is taller than other towers, a precipice deeper than the common precipice or a famous painting particularly large or small, that is all right, for the difference can be ascertained and talked about; it is for this reason that they tend to seek out a famous palace that is particularly spacious or particularly old, and among landscapes they prefer the wild ones. If you could only trick them about train schedules, hotel rates, and uniforms (but that is just what they would never fall for!), and set them down unawares on a cliff in the Saxon Switzerland, you could no doubt convince them to feel a genuine Matterhorn thrill, for surely Saxony is dizzying enough. If, however, something is not high, deep, large, small, or strikingly painted, in short, if something is not a phenomenon worth talking about, but merely beautiful, they choke—as though on a big smooth bite that will neither go up nor down, a morsel too soft to suffocate on, and too tough to let a word pass. Thus emerge those Oohs! and Ahs!, painful syllables of suffocation. You cannot very well reach with your fingers down your throat; and we have not yet found a better means of getting the necessary words out of our mouth. It isn't right to make fun of this. Such exclamations express a very painful feeling of constriction.

Experienced art commentators naturally have their own special techniques about which we might well have something to say; but this would be going too far. And, moreover, even the uncorrupted average man, despite the disagreeable effects of his constriction, feels a genuine satisfaction when standing face to face, as it were, with something that is acknowledged by experts as beautiful. This satisfaction has its own curious nuances. It contains for instance some of the same pride you feel when you can say that you passed the bank building at the very same hour when the famous bank robber X must have made his escape; other people already feel enraptured just to set foot in the city in which Goethe spent eight days, or to know the cousin by marriage of the lady who first swam the English Channel; there are indeed people who find it particularly wonderful just to live in such a momentous era. It always seems to revolve around a having-been-there; though in general it requires some element of complication, it must have an air of personal exclusivity. For as much as people lie, pretending to be completely engrossed in their occupations, they take a childish delight in personal experiences and that incalculable sense of importance that such experiences give us. It is then that they feel touched by their own "personal destiny," which is an altogether extraordinary thing: "He was just talking to me at that very moment when he slipped and broke his leg . . .!" What they feel, were they to be able to put it into words, is as if, behind that great blue window with the cloud curtains, someone had been standing a long time watching them.

And you may not want to believe it, but it is usually for this very reason alone that we ourselves travel to those places depicted in the postcards we buy, a tendency which does not in and of itself make sense, since it would after all be much easier simply to order the cards by mail. And this is the reason why such postcards have to be so overbearingly and over-realistically beautiful; if ever they were to start looking natural, then mankind would have lost something. "So this is what it looks like here," we say to ourselves and study the card mistrustfully; then we write below: "You can't imagine how lovely it is . . . !" It is the same manner of speaking by which one man confides in another: "You can't imagine how much she loves me. . . ."

Who Made You, Oh Forest Fair . . . ?

When it is very hot outside and you see a forest, you sing: "Who made you, oh forest fair, rise so tall above the ground?" This occurs with automatic certainty and is one of the reflex actions of the German nation. The more unconsciously their heat-parched tongue knocks about in their mouth, and the more like a sharkskin their throat has become, the more passionately will they gather their last strength for a musical finale, and they solemnly affirm that they will sing praises to the master above as long as their voice fills the air. This song is sung with all the obduracy of that idealism which, when all sufferings have come to an end, deserves a drink.

Yet whoever you are, you need only have been once, for an extended period of time, in the proximity of a sweltering 104° fever, at which the border between death and life begins, to drop all your scorn for this song. You lie there— assuming you have been through a serious accident, have been operated on, and are all patched up again—as a convalescent in the beautiful sanatorium of some health resort, all wrapped up in white sheets and blankets on an airy balcony, and the world is nothing but a distant hum; and chances are, if the sanatorium is so designed, you will also be bedded down in such a way that for weeks you will have nothing before your eyes but the steep, green canopy of trees hugging the side of a mountain. You become as patient as a pebble in a brook, over which the water rushes.

Your memory is still all afever, and you taste nothing but the residual sweet dryness after the anaesthesia. And you humbly remember that in the days and nights during which death and life wrestled over you and the most profound and ultimate thoughts would have been appropriate, you had absolutely nothing on your mind but the same redundant image: on a hike in high summer you are approaching the cool edge of a forest. Again and again this illusion returns, stepping out of the bilious blaze of the sun into the dampness of the dark, only to have to be thrust back again, approaching the same destination through sun-parched fields. How little do paintings, novels and philosophies count at such moments! In such a weakened state the meager remains of our corporal self close up like a feverish hand, in which our intellectual aspirations melt away like little ice cubes that cannot keep you cool. You resolve henceforth to live a life which is as ordinary as possible, replete with serious attempts to achieve affluence and its rewards, which are as simple and unchanging as the taste of coolness, pleasure, and a quiet occupation. Oh, how you abhor everything out of the ordinary, everything that demands effort and ingenuity when you are sick, and how you long for the eternal, healthy mediocrity common to all men. Is there a problem in that? Let it wait! Sometimes it is a more pressing question, whether in an hour there will be chicken broth or something more invigorating on the table, and you sing to yourself: "Who made you, oh forest fair, rise so tall above the ground? . . . " Life seems bent so strangely straight; since, by the way, you never could keep a tune before.

But little by little your recovery proceeds, and with it the evil spirit of the intellect returns. You start observing things. Directly opposite your balcony that green canopy of trees still hugs the side of a mountain, and you still hum that grateful song to it, a habit which all of a sudden you can't seem to shake; but one day you realize that the forest does not consist only of a series of notes, but of trees, which before you couldn't tell for the forest. And if you look very closely, you can even recognize how these friendly giants struggle over light and ground with the envy of horses fighting over fodder. They stand quietly side by side, here perhaps a grove of spruce, there a grove of beech trees: It looks naturally dark and light as in a painting; and moralistically edifying as the touching togetherness of families. But, in fact, it is the eve of a thousand-year-long battle.

Are there not seasoned naturalists from whom we can learn that the stallwart oak, today a veritable epitomy of solitude, once spread in hoardes far and wide throughout Germany? That the spruce, which now supplants everything else, was a relatively recent interloper? That at some time in the past an era of the beech empire was established and, at another time, the imperialism of the alder dominated? There was a migration of the trees, just as there was a migration of the nations, and wherever you see a homogeneous native forest, it is in fact an army that established a stronghold on the embattled promontory; and where a variety of trees seem to conjure up an image of happy coexistence, they are really scattered combatants, the surviving remnants of enemy hoardes crowded together, too tired and exhausted to continue battle!

This, at any rate, is still poetry, even if it isn't quite the poetry of peacefulness which we look for in the woods; real nature is above even that. Let nature revive your strength and—insofar as all the advantages of modern nature are put at your disposal—you will likewise make the second observation that a forest consists mostly of rows of boards bedecked by a little greenery. This is no discovery, but merely an avowal of the truth; I suspect that we could not even let our glance dip into the greenery, if all were not prearranged so that our glance was met by straight and even spaces. The sly foresters arrange for a little irregularity, for a tree that steps out of line to the rear of the columns just to catch our glance, for a diagonal branch or a toppled limb left lying there all summer. For they have a subtle sense of nature and know that we would not otherwise believe them. Virgin forests have something highly unnatural and degenerate about them. The unnatural, which has become a second nature in nature, recovers its natural aspect in woods like this. A German forest wouldn't do such a thing.

A German forest is conscious of its duty, that we might sing of it: "Who made you, oh forest fair, rise so tall above the ground? May our master's praise resound, as long as my voice fills the air!" That master is a master forester, a chief forester or forest commissioner, who built up the forest in such a way that he would by all rights be very angry if we did not immediately notice his expert handiwork. He provided for the light, the air, the selection of trees, access roads, the location of the lumber camps, and the removal of the tree stumps; and gave the trees that beautiful, perfectly aligned, well-kempt appearance that so delights us when we come from the wild irregularity of the metropolis.

Behind this forest missionary, who with a simple heart preaches the gospel of the lumber business to the trees, there stands a grounds keeper, a land officer or princely appointee, who writes the rules. According to his ordinances, so many square feet of open space or young saplings are prescribed each year; he distributes the beautiful vistas and the cool shades. But it is not in his hands that the ultimate destiny of the forest lies. Still higher than this authority are the reigning woodland deities, the lumber dealers and their clients, the sawmills, wood pulp plants, building contractors, shipyards, cardboard and paper mills . . . Here the connection dissolves in that nameless chaos, the spectral flow of goods and money which accords even the man whose poverty drives him to suicide the certainty that the consequences of his act will effect the economy; and promotes you to the status of superintendant of sheep and woods, all of which can go to hell, when in the sweltering

94

big city summer your pants rub up against a wooden bench and the bench in turn rubs up against your pants.

Shall we then sing, "Who made you, oh lovely depot of technology and trade so fair, rise so tall above the ground? May our master's praise—of the termites sucking sustenance from your wood chips; but also, depending on the circumstances, other methods of your utilization—resound, as long as my voice fills the air!—?" To this question we will have to answer no, in principle. There still is the ozone that hangs over the trees, the forest's soft green substance, its coolness, its stillness, its depth and solitude. These are un-used by-products of the forester's technology and are as splendidly superfluous as man is on vacation, when he is nothing but himself. Herein lies a deep affinity. Nature's bosom may indeed be unnatural, but then man on vacation is likewise an artificial construct. He has resolved not to think about business, a resolve that constitutes a veritable inner ban of silence. After a short while everything grows unspeakably and delightfully still and empty in him.

How grateful he is, then, for the little signs, the quiet words that nature has in store for him! How lovely are those path markers, those inscriptions informing him that it is only another quarter hour's walk to the Welcome Wayfarers Inn, those benches and weathered plaques that reveal the ten commandments of the forestry commission; nature waxes eloquent! How happy is he who finds others in whose company he can tread closer to nature: partners for his card game on the lawn or a punch bowl at sunset! Through such tiny aids, nature acquires the salient qualities of a lithograph, and much of the confusion is filtered out. A mountain is then a mountain, a brook is a brook, green and blue lie with consummate clarity side by side, and no ambiguities keep the observer from coming, by the quickest route, to the conviction that it is indeed a lovely thing that he possesses.

However, as soon as we have gotten this far, the so-called eternal values easily set in. Ask any man of today, not yet confused by critical chatter, what he prefers, a landscape painting or a lithograph, and he will answer without hesitation that he prefers a good lithograph. For the uncorrupted man loves clarity and idealism, and industry is infinitely better at both than art.

Such questions reveal the progressing convalescence of our patient. The doctor says to him: "Criticize as much as you like; bad temper is a sign of recovery."—"That makes perfect sense!" replied the distressed patient, returning to consciousness.

Threatened Oedipus

> Though malicious and one-
> sided, this critique lays no claim
> to scientific objectivity.

If ancient man had his Scylla and Charybdis, so modern man his Wasserman test and Oedipus complex; for if he succeeded in eluding the former, and effectively setting a little offspring on its own two feet, he can be all the more certain that the latter will catch up with his son. It may well be said that without Oedipus, next to nothing is possible nowadays, neither family life nor architecture.

Since I myself grew up without Oedipus, I must of course apply great caution in speaking my mind on such matters, but I admire the methods of Psychoanalysis. I remember the following from my youth: when one of us boys was so heaped with insults that, even with the best of intentions, he could not think up a retort that packed an equally powerful punch, he simply resorted to the little word "yourself," which, when plugged into the silent pauses of his opponent's tirade, promptly reversed all insults and sent them back to their source. And I was very pleased to discover in my study of psychoanalytic literature that all those persons who do not believe in the infallibility of Psychoanalysis are immediately shown to have their reasons for disbelieving, reasons which can naturally only be of a psychoanalytic nature. This is splendid proof of the fact that even scientific methods were acquired before puberty.

If, however, in its use of the "riposte," medical science reminds us of the good old days of the mail coach, it does so, albeit unconsciously, certainly not without deep psychological associations. For it is one of medicine's greatest achievements that, in light of the present scarcity of time, it educates us to a more leisurely use of time, indeed to an easy squandering of this fleeting natural product. The only thing you know after having placed yourself in the hands of the "soul-improvement expert" is that someday the treatment will come to an end, but you are satisfied all the same with the inroads you make. Impatient patients are quickly relieved of their neurosis, and immediately start in on a new one, but he who has arrived at an appreciation of the true pleasure of Psychoanalysis will not be so overeager. From the hustle and bustle of everyday life you step into your friend's chamber, and if the world outside explodes with all its mechanical energies, here you find the good old time gently flowing. With solicitous care, you are asked how you slept and what you dreamed. The sense of family, otherwise so sadly neglected nowadays, is once again given its natural significance, and we learn that what Aunt Gerda said when the serving girl broke the plate is not at all ridiculous, but rather, if viewed in a proper light, more telling than one of Goethe's recorded remarks. We even may ignore the fact that it is said to be not unpleasant to speak of the "bird in our brain"—as the German saying for being crazy goes—particularly if that "bird" happens to be a stork. For more important than any particulars, and clearly the most important object of such treatment, is that the individual, softly hypnotically coaxed, should learn once again to feel himself to be the measure of all things. For centuries he has been told that his behavior is beholden to a culture that is much more important than he himself; and since in the last generation we finally all but rid ourselves of this culture, it was henceforth the rampant spread of innovations and inventions beside which the individual felt like a nothing: but now Psychoanalysis takes this stunted individual by the hand and shows him that all he needs is courage and healthy gonads. May this noble science never end! This is my wish as a lay amateur; but I believe this wish is consistent with that of the experts.

I am therefore disturbed by a suspicion, which may well derive from my lay ignorance, but may also be true. For as far as I know, the aforementioned Oedipus complex is now, more than ever, central to the theory; almost all symptoms are traced back to it, and I fear that within one to two generations there will be no more Oedipus! We are cognizant of the fact that he springs out of the nature of the little man, who finds his pleasure in his mother's lap, and is supposed to be jealous of his father, who drives him away from there. What, then, if the mother no longer has a lap?! We understand of course where this leads: the lap is after all not only the bodily region for which the word in its strictest sense was coined; but it also signifies psychologically the whole incubative mothering quality of the woman, the bosom, the warming fat, the calming and tender-loving softness; indeed, it signifies also, and not unjustifiably so, the skirt whose wide pleats form a secret nest. In this sense, the fundamental experiences of psychoanalysis definitely derive from the dress of the 1870s and 80s, and not from the ski outfit. And particularly if you consider the modern bathing suit: where is the lap in our day and age? If with psychoanalytic longing I attempt embryonically to imagine my way back to the lap in the running and swimming girls' and womens' bodies that are fashionable nowadays, then, their curious beauty notwithstanding, I see no reason why the next generation might not be just as eager to crawl back into the father's lap.

And what then?

Will we instead of Oedipus be given an Orestes? Or will Psychoanalysis have to give up its beneficent effect?

Unstorylike Stories

The Giant Agoag

When the hero of this little story—and truly, he was one!—
rolled up his sleeves, two arms as thin as the sound of a toy
clock came into view. And the women praised his intelligence in a friendly manner, while they went out with others
for whom they didn't always have such kind words. Just one
comely beauty once, to everyone's surprise, deigned to grant
him a greater intimacy; she loved to make big eyes at him and
shrug her shoulders. And following the vacillation in the
selection of endearments that usually comes at the start of
every love affair, she called him "My little squirrel!"

Henceforth he read only the sports section of the newspaper, in the sports section dwelt most avidly on the boxing
news, and of the boxing news preferred to read about the
heavyweights.

His life was not happy; but he never stopped searching
for a means to build up his strength. And since he didn't
have enough money to join a muscle-building club, and
since sports has in any case, according to the modern view,
long since ceased to be the lowly talent of the body, and has
become instead a moral triumph, a victory of the spirit, he
pursued the search for strength on his own. There was no
free afternoon which he did not use to go walking on his

toes. Whenever he found himself alone and unobserved in a room, he reached with his right hand behind his shoulder to grab the things that lay on his left, and vice versa. Getting dressed and undressed became a challenge to the spirit which he carried out in the most strenuous way possible. And since every muscle in the human body has a counter muscle, such that one stretches while the other flexes, or flexes while the other stretches, he succeeded in infusing every movement with the most unspeakable difficulties. One might well maintain that on good days he consisted of two people, complete strangers who were forever fighting with each other. And when, after such an optimally utilized day, he got ready to go to sleep, he once again strained all at once, all the muscles he could reach; and then he lay there, in his own muscles, like an alien piece of meat in the claws of a bird of prey, until tiredness overcame him, his grip loosened, and he let himself slip vertically into sleep. By this lifestyle it was inevitable that one day he would become invincibly strong. But before this could happen, he got into a fight on the street and was beaten up by a sizable crowd.

Following this disgraceful melee, in which his soul suffered injury, he was never the same as before, and it was questionable for quite some time thereafter if he would be able to endure a life stripped of all hope. Then he was saved by a giant omnibus. He chanced to witness a massive omnibus run over a rather athletically built young man, and this accident, as tragic as it turned out for the victim, resulted in a new point of departure in his life. The athlete was, so to speak, peeled off existence like a wood shaving or the skin of an apple; whereas the omnibus, hardly stirred by the contact, rolled to the side, stopped and gaped back out of its many eyes. It was a sad sight, but our man quickly saw his chance and climbed aboard the victor.

So it was and so from that hour it would remain: for fifteen cents he could, whenever he wished, crawl into the body of a giant from whose path every muscleman had to jump aside. The giant's name was Agoag. That probably stood for Athletes-Get-on-Omnibus-Associated Group; and in any case, those who still want to experience fairy tales nowadays can't be too overly cautious. So our hero climbed on top of the bus and was so big that he lost any feeling for the dwarves that swarmed on the street below. He could no longer even imagine what they had to talk about with each other. He loved to see them leap aside in terror. And when they crossed the line of traffic, he barked at them like a watchdog snapping at sparrows. Cognizant of his destructive power, he looked down disdainfully on the roofs of the stylish private cars whose elegance had always in the past intimidated him, and he felt like a man with a knife eyeing the poor dumb chickens in a coop. This didn't require that much imagination, just the application of a little logic. For if it is true what they say, that clothes make the man, then why not an omnibus too? You put its immense strength on about you, like someone else might put on a suit of armor or hang a rifle over his shoulder; and if knightly valor can be associated with armor, then why not just as well with an omnibus? And even for the mighty conquerors of history: was it their weak body softened by the comforts of power that instilled terror in the enemy, or the apparatus of power with which they were able to surround themselves that made them invincible? And what is it, our man thought (enthroned in his new way of thinking), about the noble coterie who surround the kings of boxing, running and swimming like courtiers, from manager to trainer to the man who carries away the bucket of bloody water or lays the bathrobe on the champ's shoulders; do these contemporary descendants of the the old Lord High Steward and Cup-Bearer derive their dignity from their own power, or from the reflected rays of an alien power that surrounds them? (As one can see, he drew great insight from the accident.)

From now on, he no longer used every free moment for sports, but rather for bus riding. He dreamed of acquiring a far-reaching long-distance bus pass. And if he did in fact fulfill his dream and hasn't since died, been crushed or run over, didn't fall from a precipice, or land in a madhouse, then he is still riding around with it today. Once, though, he went too far and took a girlfriend along for the ride, expecting that she would be able to appreciate intellectual masculine beauty. There with them in the massive belly of the bus was a miniscule parasite with a mustache who smiled a few times suggestively at his girlfriend, and she, almost imperceptibly, smiled back; and when this mustached mite got up to leave, he even accidentally brushed past her and seemed to whisper something in her ear while publically offering chivalrous apologies. Our hero boiled with rage; he would have liked to jump on his rival, but as small as the latter would have appeared beside the giant Agoag, just so big and brawny did he appear inside. Thus our hero remained seated and later showered his girlfriend with reproaches. But even though he had initiated her in his way of thinking, she did not reply—I don't care a hoot about musclemen, it's big husky omnibusses I love!—but rather simply lied to him.

Ever since this spiritual betrayal, to be blamed on the inferior intellectual daring of women, our hero took fewer bus rides, and when he did ride a bus, it was without any female companion. He divined a glimmering of that fateful truth about man summed up by the adage: The strong are strongest alone!

A Man without Character

You really have to seek out character with a lantern nowadays; and you would probably look ridiculous to boot, walking around in broad daylight with a burning lamp. I want to tell the story of a man who always had difficulties with his character, who, to put it plainly, never even had a character; yet I am concerned that I may simply not have recognized his significance early enough, or that he may be something like a pioneer or forerunner of a new trend.

We were neighbors as kids. Whenever he carried off one of those little feats of mischief that are so splendid you'd rather not tell about them, his mother groaned, for the beating that she gave him tired her out. "Son," she wailed, "you haven't a speck of character; what in the world will become of you!?" In serious cases, however, his father was called in, and then the beatings had a certain ceremonious aspect and a solemn dignity, something like a school assembly. Before the festivities, my friend had with his own hands to go get the Lord High Counselor a cane switch whose primary use was to beat out the wash and was kept by the cook; and when it was all over with, the son had to kiss his father's hand and, thanking him for the reprimand, had to beg forgiveness for the trouble he had caused his dear

parents. My friend did it the other way around. He pleaded
and howled for forgiveness before it began, and continued
pleading from one blow to the next; but when it was all
over with, he refused to utter another word, was all red in
the face, swallowed tears and saliva, and tried by means of
assiduous rubbing to wipe away the traces of his pain. "I
don't know,"—his father liked to say—"what will become
of that boy; the rascal has absolutely no character!"

So in our childhood, character was what you got a
beating for, even though you didn't have it. There seems to
have been a certain injustice in this. Character, my friend's
parents maintained (on one exceptional occasion when they
demanded it of him and actually sought to make him
understand), was the conceptual opposite of bad report
cards, skipping school, tin pans tied to dogs' tails, idle
chatter and clowning around during class, obstinate
excuses, faulty memory, and innocent birds struck by the
sling of a nasty little marksman. But the natural opposite
of all this was, after all, the terror of punishment, the fear
of discovery and the pangs of guilt that tormented the soul
with the remorse that you felt when things went wrong.
That was all; there was no room and no function left over
for character, and it was completely superfluous. Still, they
demanded it of us.

Perhaps the enlightening words of counsel occasionally
spoken to my friend during his punishment were supposed
to give him a basis on which to build character, advice like
"Don't you have any pride, son?!" Or: "How can anyone
be such a low-down liar?!" But I must say that I still find
it difficult to this very day to fathom how anyone is
supposed to be proud while getting a beating, or how he's
supposed to demonstrate his pride while bent over the
parental knee. Anger I can imagine; but that's just what we
weren't supposed to have! And the same holds true for lies:
How in the world are you supposed to lie, if not in a low-
down way? Awkwardly perhaps? When I think about it
today, it still seems to me as though what they really
demanded back then was for us boys to be ingenuous liars.

But thus we were charged with conflicting orders: first, don't lie; and second, if you have to lie, don't lie like a liar. Maybe grown-up criminals have mastered this, since in the courtroom it is always held as a particularly dastardly villainy if they committed their crime cold-bloodedly, with malice and forethought; but it was definitely too much to ask of us boys. I am afraid that the only reason I don't have such a marked absence of character as my friend is that I was not brought up with such painstaking care.

The most plausible of the parental dicta concerning our character was the one that joined its regrettable absence to the warning that we would have need of it as grown men: "And a boy like that wants to become a man!?"is approximately the way it went. The fact notwithstanding that this business about wanting was not altogether clear, the rest at least gave us to believe that character was something that we would only be needing later on; so why all these hurried preparations now? This would have accorded altogether with our own way of looking at it.

Even though my friend possessed no character at the time, he did not suffer from the lack of it. That only came later, and began between our sixteenth and seventeenth year. It was then that we started frequenting the theater and reading novels. My friend's brain, more prone to the dazzling seductions of art than my own, was naively annexed by the villain of the state theater, by the gentle father, the heroic lover, the comic characters, and even the devlish and bewitching femme fatale. Now he only spoke with false inflections, but suddenly possessed all the character of the German stage. If he promised something, you never knew whether you had his word as hero or villain; sometimes he started out perfidious and ended up honest, or the other way around; he would greet us friends with a grumble of displeasure only to switch suddenly to the bon vivant and offer us chocolate bonbons and a chair, or else hug us with fatherly affection and meanwhile steal the cigarettes out of our pocket.

109

And yet all this was harmless and honest compared to the effects of reading novels. Novels contain descriptions of the most amazing modes of behavior for countless situations. The main drawback, however, is that the situations you actually get yourself into never accord altogether with those for which the novels have prescribed what to do and what to say. World literature is a huge depot in which millions of souls are dressed up with magnanimity, indignation, pride, love, disdain, jealousy, nobility, and meanness. If a worshipped woman steps on our feelings, we know that we are to reply with a reproachfully soulful look; if a scoundrel mistreats an orphan, we know that we are to knock him out with a single punch. But what are we supposed to do if the worshipped woman slams her door shut in our face so that our soulful look never reaches her? Or if a table laden with costly crystal separates us from the scoundrel mistreating the orphan? Shall we break the door down just to cast our sensitive look through the splinters; and should we carefully remove the costly crystal before resorting to the indignant blow? In such truly crucial situations, literature always leaves you in the lurch; maybe things will only get better in a few hundred years, when more facets of life are described.

Meanwhile, however, the well-read character always finds himself in a particularly unpleasant fix every time he gets into a so-called real life situation. He is seething with a good dozen prescribed lines, half-raised eyebrows or clenched fists, backs turned and heaving breasts, all of which don't really fit the provocation, and yet are not altogether out of place. The corners of the mouth are simultaneously drawn upwards and downwards, the forehead both darkly furrowed and brightly illumined, and the eyes want at the same time to lunge forward reproachfully and draw back ashamedly into their sockets: this is very unpleasant, for one hurts oneself in the process from all angles. The result all too often is that familiar palpitation and heaving which spreads across the lips, eyes, hands, and throat, sometimes consuming the entire body to such an extent that it twists like a screw that has lost its nut.

It was then that my friend discovered how much more convenient it would be to possess a single character, his own, and started searching for it.

But he stumbled into new exploits. I met him again years later when he had entered the legal profession. He wore glasses, was clean-shaven and spoke in a quiet tone of voice. "You're looking me over?" he remarked. I could not deny it, something impelled me to seek an answer in his appearance. "Do I look like a lawyer?" he asked. I did not wish to disagree. He explained: "Lawyers have a very particular way of glancing over the rim of their glasses, which is different from the way, say, doctors do it. It might also be maintained that all their words and gestures are more pointed or sharp-edged than the rotund and knotty words and gestures of the theologian. The latter differ from the former as a piece of light journalism from a sermon. In brief, just as fish do not fly from tree to tree, so lawyers are submerged in a medium they never leave."

"Professional character!" I said. My friend was pleased. "It wasn't so easy," he added. "When I started out, I wore a Christ-like beard; but my boss forbade it, as it did not accord with the character of a lawyer. Thereafter I comported myself like a painter, and when that was denied me, like a sailor on shore leave." "For God's sake, what for?" I asked. "Because I naturally wanted to resist adopting a professional character," he replied. "The unfortunate thing is that you can't avoid it. There are of course lawyers that look like poets, and likewise poets that look like grocers, and grocers with the heads of thinkers. But they all have something of a glass eye or a false beard about them, or a wound that hasn't quite healed. I don't know why, but it's like that, isn't it?" He smiled as he was wont to and added resignedly: "As you know, I don't even possess a personal character. . . ."

I reminded him of his many theatrical characters. "That

was only youth?" he proceded with a sigh. "When you become a man you take on, in addition, a sexual, a national, a state, a class, and a geographical character to boot, you have a handwriting character, a character of the lines in your hand, of the shape of your skull, and if possible, a character that derives from the constellation of the stars at the moment of your birth. All that is too much for me. I never know which of my characters to follow." Once again, his quiet smile appeared: "Happily I have a fiancée who claims I do not possess the slightest trace of a character, because I have not yet kept my promise to marry her. I'll marry her for that very reason, since I can't do without her healthy judgment." "Who is your fiancée?"

"From the point of view of which character? But you know," he interrupted himself, "she still always knows what she wants! She used to be a charmingly helpless little girl—I have known her for a long time already—but she learned a lot from me. When I lie, she finds it awful; when I don't leave on time for the office in the morning, she claims I'll never be able to support a family; when I can't resolve to keep a promise I previously made, she knows that only a scoundrel could do such a thing."

My friend smiled again. He was an amiable fellow in those days, and everyone looked affectionately down on him. No one ever thought for a moment he would amount to anything. His external appearance alone already gave him away, for as soon as he started talking, every part of his body twisted into a different position; his eyes shifted to the side; shoulder, arm, and hand turned in opposite directions; and at least one leg swayed in the hollow underside of his knee like a postage scale. As I said, he was an amiable fellow back then, modest, shy, respectful; and sometimes he was also the opposite of all that, but one remained well-disposed toward him, out of curiosity alone.

When I met him again, he had a car, that woman as a wife who was now his shadow, and a respected, influential position. How he started this, I don't know; but I suspect that the secret of it all was that he grew fat. His daunted, lissom face was gone. To be more precise, it was still there, but it lay buried under a thick upholstery of flesh. His eyes, which in the old days, when he had done some mischief, could be as touching as those of a sad little monkey, had in fact not lost their internal lustre; but they had a hard time shifting sideways beneath the bulk of his heavily upholstered cheeks, and so stared forwards with a haughty, pained expression. Internally, his movements continued to twist in every which way, but on the outside, at his elbows, knees and joints, padded pillows of fat held them back, and what came out gave an impression of brusqueness and decisiveness. So he had also become the man to suit the image. His flickering soul had taken on solid walls and convictions. Sometimes a spark of his old self still sallied forth; yet it no longer emanated any brightness in the man, but was rather a shot that he gave off to impress or to achieve a specific goal. The fact is that he had forfeited much of what he was before. Above all, the things he said, it was six of one or half a dozen of the other, even if they were a half-dozen sound, reliable goods. He recalled the past as one does a youthful indiscretion.

Once I succeeded in directing his attention back to our old topic of conversation, character. "I am convinced that the development of character has something to do with the way we wage war," he expounded in short-breathed, insistent syllables, "and that nowadays, for that very reason, it can only be found among savages. For those who fight with knives and spears require character to come out on top. But what kind of character, however resolute, can stand up to tanks, flame throwers and poison gas!? What we therefore need today is discipline, not character!"

I had not contradicted him. But the strange thing was— and that's why I permit myself to record this memory—all the while he spoke and I watched him, I retained the impression that the old person was still inside him. He stood inside himself, confined within the larger fleshy revision of the old self. His gaze was stuck inside the gaze of that other, his speech inside his speech. It was almost uncanny. I have since run into him again on several other occasions, and each time had the same impression. It was clear to me, if I may say so, that he would have liked to be himself again; but something held him back.

A Story Over Three Centuries

1729

When the Marquis d'Epatant was thrown to the beasts of prey—a story which unfortunately is not mentioned in a single one of the chronicles of the 18th-century—he suddenly found himself in a tight scrape, the like of which he had never encountered. He had bid life adieu, and smiling with a look that seemed to emanate from two cleanly cut diamonds, but no longer saw anything, he stepped into nothingness. Yet this nothingness did not cause him to dissolve in eternity, but rather congealed around him in a very actual fashion; in short, not nothingness, but nothing followed, and as soon as he once again used his eyes to see, he noticed a big beast of prey watching him irresolutely. This would not, we must assume, have further ruffled the Marquis—he was afraid, but knew how to comport himself—had he not at that same instant realized that it was a female beast standing before him.

Strindbergian views were not yet current at the time; people lived and died with their 18th-century views, and Epatant's most natural response would have been to doff his hat and gallantly bow. But then he noticed that the wrists of the lady looking at him were almost as wide as his thigh, and the teeth that became visible in that voluptuous and eagerly opened mouth gave him an inkling of the massacre that awaited him. This creature that stood before him was terrifying, beautiful, strong, but absolutely feminine in her expression and bearing. The ardently playful intent evident in every limb of the wildcat's body reminded him in all respects of the ravishing, silent eloquence of love. Not only did he have to suffer dread, but he likewise had to contend with the shameful struggles that this dread waged with his masculine need, under any circumstances, to impress a female, to subdue and vanquish the woman in him. Instead of subduing her, however, he felt himself perplexed and defeated by his opponent. The female beast intimidated the beast in him, and the consummately feminine aspect that every one of her movements exuded added the stun of impotence to the failure of any resistance. He, the Marquis d'Epatant, had been reduced to the condition and role of a woman, and this in the last minute of his life! He saw no way to evade this awful affront, lost control of himself, and fortunately, no longer knew what happened to him.

2197 before Our Time

It should not be presumed that the date is correct, but if the State of the Amazons did indeed exist, then ladies to be reckoned with must have lived there. For if they had merely constituted a somewhat violently inclined women's rights organization, they would have earned the historical reputation of Abderites or Sancho Panzas, and would have remained down to the present day a comic example of unwomanly behavior. Instead, however, they live on in heroic memory, from which we may conclude that in their day they had quite a considerable reputation for burning, murdering, and looting. More than one Indo-germanic man must have been afraid of them for them to have achieved such a name for themselves. More than one hero must have run away from them. In short, they must have done no small damage to the pride of prehistoric man, until finally, to excuse so much cowardice, he made legendary figures out of them, following the same law by which a vacationer who runs from a cow will always claim it was at least an ox.

But what if this nation of virgins never existed? And this is more than likely, for the simple reason that it would be difficult to imagine divisions and regiments of storks flying new recruits in to the man-killing virgins. What, then, were the ancient heroes afraid of? Was the whole thing nothing but a curious, violently inclined dream? We cannot help but recall that classical man also venerated goddesses by whom, in the frenzy of worship, they were torn to pieces, and the Thebans knowingly visited the Sphinx like the fly visits the spider. We must shamefully wonder just a little at what kind of spider and insect dreams were harbored by these ancestors of our classical training! Exemplary athletes who didn't think much of women, they dreamed of women whom they could fear. Is it possible in the end that Mr. Sacher-Masoch should have had such a long lineage? This is hardly likely. For we may wish to imagine that the past was dark, so that today things seem all the brighter; but it is hard to believe that there should be something so deranged at the very base of our humanistic education. Were they jokers, those ancient Greeks? Or were they given to vast exaggeration, in the manner of all Levantines? Or did a primal harmlessness underlie their primal perversity, that only much later took root in our sick souls?

Dark are the early days of civilization.

1927

What have two centuries of "Modern Time" made of this story?

In open combat, a man defeats the Amazon horde and the Amazon falls in love with her conqueror. So now things are back to normal! Her obstinacy subdued, she lets her shield and spear fall, and the men, flattered in their vanity, snigger all around. This is all that's left of the old legend. Of the wild young woman marauder burning to dig the tip of her arrow into man's ribs, the age of the enlightened middle class has preserved only the moral example, namely, how unnatural drives revert back into natural urges; and perhaps also at best the paltry remains in theaters, in movies, and in the heads of sixteen-year-old bon vivants, where the demonic female, the femme fatale, and the vamp remind us from afar of their man-killing ancestresses.

But times keep changing. We will not here speak about female office managers around whom the male subordinate creeps like lowly ivy around the mighty oak; there are instances that cut closer to the core of masculine pride. Such an instance took place some time ago when the famous researcher Quantus Negatus participated in a conference at which the opposition was led by women. It was not exactly a political conference, but nonetheless, one of those at which new ideas clash with old. Quantus, a man proud of his achievements, sat comfortably ensconced in the pillows of the old. He had absolutely no intention of arguing over attitudes and greeted the presence of the ladies above all as a diverting change. While they expounded above, he eyed their feet in their flat-heeled shoes below. But suddenly he was struck by a detail: he heard them say that the men of the majority were asses. They said it in a ravishing fashion, and not exactly using this word, but all the same without that degree of respect. And when one of them sat down, another stood up relaxed and ready to repeat the accusation in a slightly different way. Little perpendicular folds of anger and effort formed on their foreheads; their gesticulations were pedantic, as when one is forced to make clear to children what lazyheads they are; and their sentences were painstakingly articulated, the way a skilled chef carves pheasant.

The famous researcher Negatus smiled; he was no ass, he stood above the situation and could open-mindedly permit himself to be taken in by its charm; when it came to the voting, his own views would of course be approved. By chance, however, he happened to cast an untimely glance at the other gentlemen of the majority. And all at once it seemed to him as if the lot of them sat there stiff-backed, like so many little women, who, faced with a man's attempt to teach them the overpowering magic of logic, can find no other weapon in their defense than to reply to each new conclusion, But I don't want to! Then he realized for the first time that he was no different from the rest. With a wandering eye, he examined legs and fingertips, the line of lips and shapely bodily curves, and yet all the while he had to hear how his power of volition had fallen asleep, and his intelligence was that of a fat bourgeois who doesn't like to exercise it much. And then something happened that in fact rarely happens, Quantus felt himself half convinced. When he thought of his reputation as a scholar, he seemed to himself like a proper housewife who fiddles around with bottles and pots at home, while these ladies leaped on a sparkling steed through the wide-open world. There were of course a number of particular things about which few people knew as much as he did; but what good was this knowledge in the face of such general questions, whose uncertainty required, he was about to say, the certainty of a whole man?! Already he sensed that the arguments his reason came up with to counter the sly contentions of these young women were actually shaky, and his thoughts followed with an almost girlish enthusiasm the wild leaps of their intellect.

What kept him composed was the fact that in the opposition camp, men likewise got up to blubber incoherencies. As a result of this, the conference sometimes became downright lively, and no one let the other finish speaking. Quantus Negatus observed what the female speakers did: in this chaotic din of masculine clamor, they smiled in silence and it seemed to him that they gave a plaintive sign. Then each time a corpulently hefty young man with a wide face and a thick head of hair got up and gave off a veritable booming phenomenon of voice, he in turn was interrupted by loud exclamations that made little sense, but in one burst swept twenty contentious voices over the crowd, so that in the silence that followed you could once again hear the interrupted female speakers. "That's a man!" Negatus thought, flattered at first. But when he reflected more upon it, in the mood he was in at that moment, he realized that a powerful voice was after all just another sensual phenomenon, like a long pigtail or an opulent bosom had been in his youth. These thoughts, so foreign to his usual way of thinking, tired him out. He was more than a little bit tempted to leave his party in the lurch and sneak out of the gathering. Dark memories from his high school days stirred in him: the Amazons? "What a topsy-turvy world!" he thought. But then he also thought: "How curious it is, for once, to imagine a topsy-turvy world. It provides a certain change of pace." This train of thought made him feel confident again; there was a certain boldness in it, a candid, manly curiosity. "How dark is the future of civilization!" he thought. "I am a man, but that will finally mean something very feminine, if we don't soon return to an age of true men!" But when the issue was brought to a vote he sided after all with the reaction.

The opposition was defeated; the conference came to an end. Quantus stirred awake, and with a courtly bad conscience, his eyes searched for those of his tenacious female opponents. But they were just then in the process of powdering their faces and had pulled out their little silver mirrors. With the same unerring detachment with which before they uttered such deadly words, they now applied their powder. Quantus was astonished. And his last, albeit still highly disconcerted, thought upon leaving was this: "Why do comely male heads trouble themselves over such useless thoughts?!"

Children's Story

Mr. Hiff, Mr. Haff, and Mr. Huff went out hunting together. And because it was autumn, nothing grew in the fields; nothing but earth that had been so loosened by the plough that their boots got brown all the way up to the leg. There was an awful lot of earth all around, nothing but still brown waves as far as the eye could see; sometimes one of those waves wore a cross on its crest, or a saint or a deserted pathway; it was very lonesome.

As they stepped back down into a hollow, the gentlemen spotted a hare, and because it was the first animal they had seen all day, all three raised their rifles quickly to their cheeks and fired. Mr. Hiff aimed over his right boot toe, Mr. Huff over his left, and Mr. Haff aimed right between his two boots, for the hare sat about the same distance from each of them and looked up in their direction. Now the three shots raised a terrible thunder, the three bits of buckshot rattled through the air like three clouds of hail, and the ground exploded in dust; but once nature had recovered from this shock, the hare lay there in the heap of pepper and moved no more. Only nobody knew now to whom he belonged, for all three had shot him at the same time. Mr. Hiff called out already from afar, "If the hare's hit

121

on the right, he's mine" because he shot from the left; Mr. Huff maintained the same, but from the opposite side; but Mr. Haff argued, that the hare could still have pivoted at the last moment, which could however only be established if he had been shot in the breast or the back: but then, and in any case, the hare belonged to him! When they came up close, however, they realized that it was impossible to decide where the hare had been hit, and started arguing anew about whose hare he was.

Then the hare politely raised himself upright and said: "Gentlemen, if you can't decide the matter among yourselves, then I'll take the liberty of still being alive! For I fell, as I now realize, from the mere shock of it."

Then Mr. Hiff and Mr. Haff were, as we say, all in a huff, which in the case of Mr. Huff naturally goes without saying. But the hare proceeded unperturbed. He regarded them with big, hysterical eyes—probably, after all, because death had grazed his hide—and began to tell the hunters their fortunes. "Gentlemen, I can prophecy your end," he said, "if only you let me live! You, Mr. Hiff, will in as soon as seven years and three months be mowed down by death in the form of a bull's horns; and Mr. Haff will grow very old, but I see an awfully grisly end for you—something— well, it isn't so easy to talk about." He paused and regarded Haff with a look of concern, then snapped out of it and rattled off quickly: "But Mr. Huff will choke on a peach pit, that's simple."

Then the hunters turned pale, and the wind howled in over this lonely place. But as the gun barrels still rattled in the wind against their legs, their fingers loaded up their guns again, and they said: "How can you know what hasn't happened yet, you liar!"

"The bull that is supposed to spear me in seven years," said Mr. Hiff, "isn't even born yet; how can he spear me if he may never be born!?"

And Mr. Huff consoled himself in this way, saying: "All I have to do is not eat any more peaches, and already you're a swindler!"

122

But Mr. Haff just said: "Well, well!"

The hare replied: "You gentlemen can make of this what you will; it won't do you any good."

Then the hunters made ready to trample the hare to death with their boots, and yelled: "No hare is going to make us superstitious!!" But in that instant an ugly old hag came walking by, carrying a load of kindling, and the hunters had to spit three times quickly so as to ward off the evil eye.

Then the hag, who had noticed what they'd done, grew angry and cried back: "Yas tink I couldn' toin der heads in de old days!" No one could say for sure where her accent was from; but it sounded an awful lot like the dialect of Hell.

The hare took advantage of this opportunity to escape.

The hunters thundered after him with their rifles, but the hare was no more to be seen, and the old hag had also disappeared; though they thought they heard a wild cackle above the sound of the three shots.

Then Mr. Haff wiped the sweat off his brow and shivered.

Mr. Hiff said: "Let's go home."

And Mr. Huff was already bounding up the hill.

When they got to the stone cross up on the top of the hill though, they felt safe in the proximity and took a rest.

"We made fools of ourselves," said Mr. Huff, "—it was an absolutely ordinary hare."

"But he spoke to us—" said Mr. Haff.

"That can only have been the wind, or the blood climbing to our ears," Mr. Hiff and Mr. Huff explained.

Then God whispered down from the stone cross: "Thou shalt not kill. . . !"

The three were once again struck with terror and stepped back a good twenty steps from the stone cross; things are bad when you can't even feel safe here! And before they could say another word, they found themselves bounding home with giant steps. It was only after the familiar smoke of their rooftops curled round the bushes, and the village dogs barked and children's voices shot through the air like the chirp of sparrows that their legs stopped shaking. They stood still on them, feeling warm and safe. "Everybody's got to die of something," sighed Mr. Haff, who according to the hare's prophecy had the longest to live; he knew damn well why he'd said what he said, though all of a sudden he grew troubled by the suspicion that his pals might also know why, and he was ashamed to ask them.

But Mr. Hiff replied in kind: "If I weren't allowed to kill, well then I wouldn't be allowed to be killed either, would I? Ergo, I say, there's a fundamental contradiction here!" Each might apply this as he saw fit, a sensible answer it was not, and Mr. Hiff chuckled philosophically, so as to hide the fact that he was dying to know if the others had understood him all the same, or if something wasn't right in his head.

Mr. Huff, the third one, pensively trampled an earthworm underfoot and replied: "We don't only kill animals, we also protect them and preserve order in the field."

Then everyone knew that the others knew too; and while everyone secretly remembered it, the experience already began to fade like a dream after waking, for what three men heard and saw cannot be a secret and thereafter not a miracle either, but must at best be a delusion. And all three suddenly sighed: Thank God! Mr. Hiff sighed it over his left boot toe, Mr. Huff over his right, for both squinted back at God in the field, whom they secretly thanked for not having actually appeared in person; but since the two others looked aside, Mr. Haff could turn himself all the way around to the cross, twitch his ears, and say: "We drank brandy on an empty stomach today, a hunter shouldn't ever do that."

"That's it!" all three agreed, sang a merry hunter's song about green woods and fields, and tossed stones at a cat that had surreptitiously slipped into the field to hunt hare eggs; for now the hunters were no longer afraid of the hare. But this last part of the story may not be quite as authentic as the rest, for there are people who claim that hares lay eggs on Easter.

The Blackbird

The two men whom I must mention in order to relate three little stories, in which the narrative pivots around the identity of the narrator, were friends from youth; let's call them Aone and Atwo. The fact is that such early friendships grow ever more astounding the older you get. You change over the years, from the crown of your head to the soles of your feet, from the skin's soft down to the depths of your heart, but strangely enough, your relationship with each other stays the same, fluctuating about as little as the communion we each carry on with that diverse host of sirs successively addressed as *I*. It is beside the point whether or not you still identify with that little blond numskull photographed once long ago; as a matter of fact, you can't really say for sure that you even like the little devil, that bundle of I. And so too, you may very well both disagree with and disapprove of your best friends; indeed, there are many friends who can't stand each other. And in a certain sense, those friendships are the deepest and the best, for without any admixtures, they contain that indefinable essence in its purest form.

The youth that united the two friends Aone and Atwo was nothing less than religious in character. While both were brought up in an institution that prided itself on the proper emphasis it placed on the religious fundamentals, the pupils of that institution did their best to ignore those selfsame principles. The school chapel, for instance, was a real, big, beautiful church, complete with a stone steeple; it was reserved for the school's exclusive use. The absence of strangers proved a great boon, for while the bulk of the student body was busy according to the dictates of sacred custom, now kneeling, now rising at the pews up front, small groups could gather at the rear to play cards beside the confessional booths, or to smoke on the organ steps. And some escaped up the steeple, whose pointed spire was ringed by a saucer-like balcony on the stone parapet of which, at a dizzying height, acrobatics were performed that could easily have cost the lives of far less sin-burdened boys than these.

One such provocation of the Lord involved a slow, muscle-straining elevation of the feet in midair, while with glance directed downwards, you grasped the parapet, balancing precariously on your hands. Anyone who has ever tried this stunt on level ground will appreciate just how much confidence, bravery, and luck are required to pull it off on a foot-wide stone strip up at the top of a tower. It must also be said that many wild and nimble boys, though virtuoso gymnasts on level ground, never did attempt it. Aone, for instance, never tried it. Atwo, on the other hand—and let this serve to introduce him as narrator—was, in his boyhood the creator of this test of character. It was hard to find another body like his. He didn't sport an athletic build like so many others, but seems to have developed muscles naturally, effortlessly. A narrow small-ish head sat atop his torso, with eyes like lightning bolts wrapped in velvet, and teeth that one would sooner have associated with the fierceness of a beast of prey than the serenity of a mystic.

Later, during their student days, the two friends professed a materialist philosophy of life devoid of God or the soul, viewing man as a physiologic or economic machine—

which in fact he may very well be, though this wasn't the point as far as they were concerned: since the appeal of such a philosophy lies, not in its inherent truth, but rather in its demonic, pessimistic, morbidly intellectual character. By this time their relationship had already become that special kind of friendship. And while Atwo studied forestry, and spoke of traveling as a forest ranger to the far reaches of Russia or Asia, as soon as he was through with his studies, his friend Aone, who scorned such boyish aspirations, had by then settled on a more solid pursuit, and had at the time already cast in his lot with the rising labor movement. And when they met again shortly before the great war, Atwo already had his Russian adventure behind him. He spoke little about it, was now employed in the offices of some large corporation, and seemed, despite the appearance of middle-class comfort, to have suffered considerable disappointments. His old friend had in the meantime left the class struggle and become editor of a newspaper that printed a great deal about social harmony and was owned by a stock broker. Henceforth the two friends despised each other insuperably, but once again fell out of touch; and when they finally met again for a short while, Atwo told the following story the way one empties out a sack of memories for a friend, so as to be able to push on again with a clean bill of lading. It matters little under the circumstances how the other responded, and their exchange can perhaps best be related in the form of a monologue. It would be far more important to the fabric of the tale were it possible to describe exactly what Atwo looked like at the time (which is easier said than done), for this raw impression of the man is not without bearing on the gist of his words. Suffice it to say that he brought to mind a sharp, taut, and narrow riding crop balanced on its soft tip, leaning up against the wall; it was in just such a half-erect, half-slouching posture that he seemed to feel most at ease.

Among the most extraordinary places in the world—said Atwo—are those Berlin courtyards where two, three, or four buildings flash their rear ends at each other, and where, in square holes set in the middle of the walls, kitchen maids sit and sing. You can tell by the look of the red copper pots hung in the pantry how loud their clatter is. From far down below a man's voice bawls curses up at one of the girls, or heavy wooden shoes go clip clop back and forth across the cobblestones. Slowly. Heavily. Incessantly. Senselessly. Forever. Isn't it so?

The kitchens and bedrooms look outwards and downwards on all this; they lie close together like love and digestion in the human anatomy. Floor upon floor, the conjugal beds are stacked up one on top of the other; since all the bedrooms occupy the same space in each building—window wall, bathroom wall, and closet wall prescribe the placement of each bed almost down to the half yard. The diningrooms are likewise piled up floor on floor, as are the white-tiled baths and the balconies with their red awnings. Love, sleep, birth, digestion, unexpected reunions, troubled and restful nights are all vertically aligned in these buildings like the columns of sandwiches at an automat. In middle-class apartments like these your destiny is already waiting for you the moment you move in. You will admit that human freedom consists essentially of where and when we do what we do, for what we do is almost always the same: thus the sinister implications of one uniform blueprint for all. Once I climbed up on top of a cabinet just to make use of the vertical dimension, and I can assure you that the unpleasant conversation in which I was involved looked altogether different from that vantage point.

Atwo laughed at the memory and poured himself a drink; Aone thought about how they were at that very moment seated on a balcony with a red awning that belonged to his apartment, but he said nothing, knowing all too well what he might have remarked.

I am still perfectly willing to admit today, by the way—Atwo added of his own accord—that there is something awe-inspiring about such uniformity. And in the past this sense of vastness, of a wasteland, brought to mind a desert

or an ocean; a Chicago slaughterhouse (as much as the image may turn my stomach) is after all quite different from a flower pot! But the curious thing was that during the time I occupied that apartment, I kept thinking of my parents. You recall that I had almost lost contact with them—but then all of a sudden this thought came to me out of nowhere: they gave you your life. And this ridiculous thought kept coming back again and again like a fly that refuses to be shooed away. There's nothing more to be said about this sanctimonious notion ingrained in us in early childhood. But whenever I looked over my apartment, I would say to myself: there, now you've bought your life, for so and so many marks a month rent. And sometimes maybe I also said: now you've built up a life for yourself with your own two hands. My apartment served as some odd amalgamation of a warehouse, a life insurance policy and a source of pride. And it seemed so utterly strange, such an inscrutable mystery that there was something which had been given to me whether I wanted it or not; and, moreover, that that something functioned as the very foundation of everything else. And I believe that that banal thought concealed a wealth of abnormity and unpredictability, all of which I had kept safely hidden from myself. And now comes the story of the nightingale.

It began on one evening much like any other. I'd stayed home, and after my wife had gone to bed, I sat myself down in the study; the only difference that night was that I didn't reach for a book or anything else, but this too had happened before. After one o'clock the street starts getting quieter; conversations become a rarity; it is pleasant to follow the advent of evening with your ear. At two o'clock all the clamor and laughter below have clearly tipped over into intoxication and lateness. I realized that I was waiting for something, but I didn't know what for. By three o'clock— it was May—the sky grew lighter; I felt my way through the dark apartment to the bedroom and lay down without a sound. I expected nothing more now but sleep, and that the next morning would bring a day like the one that had just passed. And soon I no longer knew whether I was awake or asleep.

In the space between the curtains and the blind a dark greenness gushed forth; thin bands of the white froth of morning seeped in between the slats. This might have been my last waking impression or a suspended dream vision. Then I was awakened by something drawing near; sounds were coming closer. Once, twice I sensed it in my sleep. Then they sat perched on the roof of the building next door and leaped into the air like dolphins. I could just as well have said, like balls of fire at a fireworks display, for the impression of fireballs lingered; in falling, they exploded softly against the windowpanes and sank to the earth like great silver stars. Then I experienced a magical state; I lay in my bed like a statue on a sarcophagus cover, and I was awake, but not like during the day. It is very difficult to describe, but when I think back, it is as though something had turned me inside out; I was no longer a solid, but rather a something sunken in upon itself. And the air was not empty, but of a consistency unknown to the daylight senses, a blackness I could see through, a blackness I could feel through, and of which I too was made. Time pulsed in quick little fever spasms. Why should something not happen now that normally never happens?—It's a nightingale singing outside!—I said half aloud to myself.

Well, maybe there are more nightingales in Berlin than I thought—Atwo continued. At the time I believed that there were none in this stony preserve, and that this one must have flown to me from far away. To me!—I felt it and sat up with a smile. A bird of paradise! So it does indeed exist!—At such a moment, you see, it seems perfectly natural to believe in the supernatural; it is as if you'd spent your childhood in an enchanted kingdom. And I immediately decided: I'll follow the nightingale. Farewell, my beloved!—I thought—farewell, my beloved, my house, my city. . . ! But before I had even gotten up out of bed, and before I had figured out whether to climb up to the nightingale on the rooftop, or to follow it on the street down below, the bird had gone silent and apparently flown away.

Now he's singing from some other rooftop for the ears of another sleeper, Atwo mused.—You're probably thinking that this was the end of the story?—But it was only the beginning, and I have no idea what end it will take!

I'd been abandoned, left behind with a heavy heart. That was no nightingale, it was a blackbird, I said to myself—just as you'd like to say to me right now. Everyone knows that such blackbirds imitate other birds. By this time I was wide awake and the silence bored me. I lit a candle and considered the woman who lay next to me. Her body had the color of pale bricks. The white border of the blanket lay over her skin like a lip of snow. Wide shadow lines of mysterious derivation ringed her body—mysterious even though they must of course have had something to do with the candle and the position of my arms. So what, I thought, so what if it really was only a blackbird! The very fact that an ordinary blackbird could have had such a crazy effect on me: that makes the whole thing all the more extraordinary! For as you well know: while a single disappointment may elicit tears, a repeated disappointment will evoke a smile. And meanwhile I kept looking at my wife. This was all somehow connected, but I didn't know how. For years I've loved you—I thought to myself—like nothing else in this world, and now you lie there like a burnt-out husk of love. You're a stranger to me now, and I've arrived at the other end of love. Had I grown tired of her? I can't remember ever having felt sated. Let me put it like this, it was as if a feeling could drill its way through the heart as though through a mountain, and find another world on the other side, a world with the same valley, the same houses and the same little bridge. In all honesty, I simply had no idea what was happening. And I still don't understand it today. Perhaps it's wrong of me to tell you this story in connection with two others that happened afterwards. I can only tell you how I saw it during the experience: as a signal from afar—so it seemed to me at the time.

I lay my head beside her body that slept on unawares, and took no part in all this. Then her bosom seemed to rise and fall more strenuously than before, and the walls of the room lapped up against this sleeping form like waves against a ship far out at sea. I would probably never have been able to bring myself to say goodbye; but if I were to slip away right now, I told myself, then I'd stay the little lost boat, past which a great sturdy ship would sail unnoticing. I kissed her sleeping form, she didn't feel it. I whispered something in her ear, and maybe I did it so quietly that she wouldn't hear it. Then I ridiculed myself and sneered at the very thought of the nightingale; but quietly nonetheless I got dressed. I think that I cried, but I really did leave. I felt giddy, lighthearted, even though I tried to tell myself that no decent human being would do such a thing; I remember that I was like a drunkard rebuking the sidewalk beneath his feet to reassure himself that he's sober.

Of course, I often thought of returning; at times I would have liked to cross half the world to get back to her, but I never did. She had become untouchable to me; in short—I don't know if you understand—he who has committed an injustice and feels it down to the bone, can no longer set it aright. I am not, by the way, asking for absolution. I just want to tell you my stories to find out if they ring true. For years I haven't been able to tell them to anyone, and had I heard myself talking to myself, I would quite frankly have questioned my sanity.

Please be assured then that my reason is still the equal of your enlightened mind.

Then, two years later, I found myself in a tight fix, at the dead angle of a battle line in the south Tyrol, a line that wound its way from the bloody trenches of the Cima di Vezzena all the way to Lake Caldonazzo. There, like a wave of sunshine, the battle line dived deep into the valley, skirting two hills with beautiful names, and surfaced again on the other side, only to lose itself in the stillness of the mountains. It was October; the thinly manned trenches were covered with leaves, the lake shimmered a silent blue, the hills lay there like huge withered wreaths; like funeral wreaths, I often thought to myself without even a shudder of fear. Halting and divided, the valley spilled around them; but beyond the edge of our occupied zone, it fled such sweet diffusion and drove like the blast of a trombone: brown, broad, and heroic out into the hostile distance.

At night we pushed ahead to an advanced position, so prone now in the valley that they could have wiped us out with an avalanche of stones from above; but instead, they slowly roasted us on steady artillery fire. The morning after such a night all our faces had a strange expression that took hours to wear off: our eyes were enlarged, and our heads tilted every which way on the multitude of shoulders, like a lawn that had just been trampled on. Yet on every one of those nights I poked my head up over the edge of the trench many times, and cautiously turned to look back over my shoulder like a lover: and I saw the Brenta Mountains light blue, as if formed out of stiff-pleated glass, silhouetted against the night sky. And on such nights the stars were like silver foil cut-outs, glimmering, fat as glazed cookies; and the sky stayed blue all night; and the thin virginal moon crescent lay on her back, now silvery, now golden, basking in the splendor. You must try to imagine just how beautiful it was: for such beauty exists only in the face of danger. And then sometimes I could stand it no longer, and giddy with joy and longing, I crept out for a little nightcrawl around, all the way to the golden-green blackness of the trees, so enchantingly colorful and black, the like of which you've never seen.

But things were different during the day; the atmosphere was so easygoing that you could have gone horseback riding around the main camp. It's only when you have the time to sit back and think and to feel terror that you first learn the true meaning of danger. Every day claims its victims, a regular weekly average of so and so many out of a hundred, and already the divisional general staff officers are predicting the results as impersonally as an insurance company. You do it too, by the way. Instinctively you know the odds and feel insured, although not exactly under the best of terms. It is a function of the curious calm that you feel, living under constant crossfire. Let me add the following though, so that you don't paint a false picture of my circumstances. It does indeed happen that you suddenly feel driven to search for a particular familiar face, one that you remember seeing several days ago; but it's not there anymore. A face like that can upset you more than it should, and hang for a long time in the air like a candle's afterglow. And so your fear of death has diminished, though you are far more susceptible to all sorts of strange upsets. It is as if the fear of one's demise, which evidently lies on top of man forever like a stone, were suddenly to have been rolled back, and in the uncertain proximity of death an unaccountable inner freedom blossoms forth.

Once during that time an enemy plane appeared in the sky over our quiet encampment. This did not happen often, for the mountains with their narrow gaps between fortified peaks could only be hazarded at high altitudes. We stood at that very moment on the summit of one of those funereal hills, and all of a sudden a machine-gun barrage spotted the sky with little white clouds of shrapnel, like a nimble powder puff. It was a cheerful sight, almost endearing. And to top it off, the sun shone through the tricolored wings of the plane as it flew high overhead, as though through a stained-glass church window, or through colored crepe paper. The only missing ingredient was some music by Mozart. I couldn't help thinking, by the way, that we stood around like a crowd of spectators at the races, placing our bets. And one of us even said: better take cover! But nobody it seems was in the mood to dive like a field mouse into a hole. At that instant I heard a distant ringing drawing closer to my ecstatically upturned face. Of course, it could also have happened the other way around, that I first heard the ringing and only then became conscious of the impending danger; but I knew immediately: it's an aerial dart. These were pointed iron rods no thicker than a pencil lead that planes dropped from above in those days. And if they struck you in the skull, they came out through the soles of your feet, but they didn't hit very often, and so were soon discarded. And though this was my first aerial dart—bombs and machine-gun fire sound altogether different—I knew right away what it was. I was excited, and a second later I already felt that strange, unlikely intuition: it's going to hit!

And do you know what it was like? Not like a frightening foreboding, but rather like an unexpected stroke of good luck! I was surprised at first that I should be the only one to hear its ringing. Then I thought the sound would disappear again. But it didn't disappear. It came ever closer, and though still far away, it grew proportionally louder. Cautiously I looked at the other faces, but no one else was aware of its approach. And at that moment when I became convinced that I alone heard that subtle singing, something rose up out of me to meet it: a ray of life, equally infinite to that death ray descending from above. I'm not making this up, I'm trying to put it as plainly as I can. I believe I've held to a sober physical description so far, though I know of course that to a certain extent it's like in a dream where it seems as though you're speaking clearly, while the words come out all garbled.

It lasted a long time, during which I alone heard the sound coming closer. It was a shrill, singing, solitary, high-pitched tone, like the ringing rim of a glass; but there was something unreal about it. You've never heard anything like it before, I said to myself. And this tone was directed at me; I stood in communion with it and had not the least little doubt that something decisive was about to happen to me. I had no thoughts of the kind that are supposed to come at death's door, but all my thoughts were rather focused on the future; I can only say that I was certain that in the next second I would feel God's proximity close up to my body— which, after all, is saying quite a bit for someone who hasn't believed in God since the age of eight.

Meanwhile, the sound from above became ever more

137

tangible; it swelled and loomed dangerously close. I asked myself several times whether I should warn the others; but let it strike me or another, I wouldn't say a word! Maybe there was a devilish vanity in this illusion that high above the battlefield a voice sang just for me. Maybe God is nothing more than the vain illusion of us poor beggars who puff ourselves up in the pinch and brag of rich relations up above. I don't know. But the fact remains that the sky soon started ringing for the others too; I noticed traces of uneasiness flash across their faces, and I tell you—not one of them let a word slip either! I looked again at those faces: fellows, for whom nothing would have been more unlikely than to think such thoughts, stood there, without knowing it, like a group of disciples waiting for a message from on high. And suddenly the singing became an earthly sound, ten, a hundred feet above us and it died. He—it—was here. Right here in our midst, but closer to me, something that had gone silent and been swallowed up by the earth, had exploded into an unreal hush.

My heart beat quickly and quietly; I couldn't have lost consciousness for even a second; not the least fraction of a second was missing from my life. But then I noticed everyone staring at me. I hadn't budged an inch but my body had been violently thrust to the side, having executed a deep, one hundred-and-eighty degree bow. I felt as though I were just waking from a trance, and had no idea how long I'd been unconscious. No one spoke to me at first; then, finally, someone said: "An aerial dart!" And everyone tried to find it, but it was buried deep in the ground. At that instant a hot rush of gratitude swept through me, and I believe that my whole body turned red. And if at that very moment someone had said that God had entered my body, I wouldn't have laughed. But I wouldn't have believed it either—not even that a splinter of His being was in me. And yet whenever I think back to that incident, I feel an overwhelming desire to experience something like it again even more vividly!

I did by the way experience it one more time, but not more vividly—Atwo began his last story. He seemed to grow suddenly unsure of himself, but you could see that for that very reason he was dying to hear himself tell the story.

It had to do with his mother, for whom Atwo felt no great love, though he claimed it wasn't so.—On a superficial level, we just weren't suited to each other, he said, and that, after all, is only natural for an old woman who for decades has lived in the same small town, and a son who according to her way of thinking never amounted to much. She made me as uneasy as one would be in the presence of a mirror that imperceptibly distorts the width of one's image; and I hurt her by not coming home for years. But every month she wrote me an anxious letter, asking many questions, and even though I hardly ever wrote back, there was still something extraordinary about it; and despite all, I felt a strong tie to her, as the following incidents would soon prove.

Decades ago, perhaps, the image of a little boy had inscribed itself indelibly in her imagination—a boy in whom she may have set God knows what aspirations—this image could not thereafter be erased by any means; and since that long gone little boy happened to be me, her love clung to me, as though all the suns that have set since then were gathered somewhere, suspended between darkness and light. Here it is again: that strange vanity that is not vain. For I can assure you that I don't like to dwell on myself, nor as so many others do, to smugly stare at photographs of the person they once were, or delight in memories of what they did in such and such a place at such and such a time; this sort of savings bank account of self is absolutely incomprehensible to me. I am neither particularly sentimental, nor do I live for the moment; but when something is over and done with, then I am also over and done with that something in myself. And when on some street I happen to remember having often walked that way before, or when I see the house I used to live in, then even without thinking, I feel something like a shooting pain, an intense revulsion for myself, as though I had just been reminded of a terrible disgrace. The past drifts away as you change; and it seems to me that in whatever way you change, you wouldn't do so if that fellow you left behind had been all that flawless. But for the very reason that I usually feel this way, it was wonderful to realize that there was a person who had for my entire life preserved this image of me, an image which most likely never bore me any likeness, which nonetheless was in a certain sense the mandate of my being and my deed to life.

Can you understand me when I say that my mother was in this figurative capacity a veritable lioness, though in her real life she was locked in the persona of a manifestly limited woman? She was not bright, by our way of thinking; she could disregard nothing and came to no major conclusions about life; nor was she, when I think back to my childhood, what you'd call a good person: she was vehement and always on edge. And you can well imagine what comes from the combination of a passionate nature and limited horizons—but I would like to suggest that another kind of stature, another kind of character still exists side by side with the embodiment that human beings take on in their day-to-day existence, just as in fairy-tale times the Gods took on the forms of snakes and fish.

Not long after that incident with the aerial dart, I was taken prisoner during a battle in Russia. I consequently experienced a big change, and wasn't so quick about getting back home, since this new life appealed to me for quite a while. I still admire the socialist system, but then one day I found that I could no longer mouth a few of the essential credos without a yawn, and so I eluded the perilous repercussions by escaping back to Germany, where individualism was just reaching its inflationary peak. I got involved in all sorts of dubious business ventures, in part out of necessity, in part simply for the pleasure of being back in a good old-fashioned country, where you can misbehave and not have to feel ashamed of yourself. Things weren't going all that well for me then, and at times I'd say things were downright rotten. My parents weren't doing so

140

well either. And then my mother wrote me several times: we can't help you, son; but if the little you'll one day inherit would be of any help, then I'd wish myself dead for your sake. This she wrote to me even though I hadn't visited her in years, nor had I shown the least little sign of affection. I have to admit though that I took this for a somewhat exaggerated manner of speaking, and paid it no mind, though I didn't doubt the honesty of feeling couched in these sentimental words. But then an altogether extraordinary thing happened: My mother really did fall ill, and it appears as if she then took along my father, who was very devoted to her.

Atwo reflected—She died of an illness that she must have been carrying around in her without anyone knowing it. One might suppose that it was the confluence of numerous natural causes, and I fear that you'll think badly of me if I don't accept this explanation. But here again, the incidental circumstances proved remarkable. She definitely didn't want to die; I know for a fact that she fought it off and railed against an early death. Her will to live, her convictions, and her hopes were all set against it. Nor can it be said that a resolve of character overruled her inclinations of the moment; for if that were so, she could have thought of suicide or voluntary poverty long ago, which she by no means did. She was her own total sacrifice. But have you never noticed that your body has a will of its own? I am convinced that the sum total of what we take to be our will, our feelings and thoughts—all that seems to control us—is allowed to do so only in a limited capacity; and that during serious illness and convalescence, in critical combat, and at all turning points of fate, there is a kind of primal resolve of the entire body that holds the final sway and speaks the ultimate truth.

But be that as it may; I assure you that my mother's illness immediately gave me the impression of something self-willed. Call it my imagination, but the fact still remains that the moment I heard the news of my mother's illness, a striking and complete change came over me, even

141

though the message suggested no imminent cause for alarm. A hardness that had encompassed me melted away instantaneously; and I can say no more than that the state I now found myself in bore a great resemblance to my awakening on that night when I left my house, and to the moment of my anticipation of the singing arrow from above. I wanted to visit my mother right away, but she held me off with all sorts of excuses. At first she sent word that she looked forward to seeing me, but that I should wait out the lapse of this insignificant illness, so that she could welcome me home in good health. Later she let it be known that my visit would upset her too much for the moment. And finally, when I insisted, I was informed that recovery was imminent and that I should just be patient a little while longer. It seems as though she feared that a reunion between us might cause her to waiver in her resolve. And then everything happened so quickly, that I just barely still made it to the funeral.

I found my father likewise ailing when I got there, and as I told you, all I could do then was to help him die. He'd been a kind man in the past, but in those last weeks he was astonishingly stubborn and moody, as though he held a great deal against me and resented my presence. After his funeral I had to clear out the household, which took another few weeks; I was in no particular hurry. Now and then neighbors came by out of old force of habit, and told me just exactly where in the living room my father used to sit, where my mother would sit, and where they themselves would. They looked everything over carefully and offered to buy this or that. They're so thorough, those small town types; and once after thoroughly inspecting everything, one of them said to me: It's such a shame to see an entire family wiped out in a matter of weeks!—I of course didn't count. When I was alone, I sat quietly and read children's books; I found a big box full of them up in the attic. They were dusty, sooty, partly dried out and brittle, partly sodden from the dampness, and when you struck them they gave off an unending stream of soft black clouds; the streaked paper had worn off the cardboard bindings, leaving only jagged archipelagoes of paper behind. But as soon as I turned the pages, I swept through their contents like a sailor piloting his way across the perilous high sea, and once I made an extraordinary discovery. I noticed that the blackness at the top corner where you turned the pages and at the bottom edge of each book differed in a subtle but unmistakable way from the mildew's design, and then I found all sorts of indefinable spots, and finally, wild faded pencil markings on the title pages. And suddenly it came to me, and I realized that this impetuous disrepair, these pencil scrawls and hastily made spots were the traces of a child's fingers, my own child fingers, preserved for thirty some odd years in a box in the attic, and long forgotten!

Well, as I told you, though it may for some people not be an earth-shattering event to remember themselves, it was for me as if my life had been turned upside down. I also discovered a room that thirty and some odd years ago had been my nursery; later it was used to store linen and the like, but the room had essentially been left the way it was when I sat there at my pinewood table beneath the kerosene lamp whose chain was decorated with three dolphins. There I sat once again for many hours a day, and read like a child whose legs are too short to touch the floor. For you see, we are accustomed to an unbounded head, reaching out into the empty ether, because we have solid ground beneath our feet. But childhood means to be as yet ungrounded at both ends, to still have soft flannel hands, instead of adult pincers, to sit before a book as though perched on a little leaf soaring over bottomless abysses through the room. And at that table, I tell you, I really couldn't reach the floor.

I also set myself a bed in this room and slept there. And then the blackbird came again. Once after midnight I was awakened by a wonderful, beautiful singing. I didn't wake up right away, but listened first for a long time in my sleep. It was the song of the nightingale; she wasn't perched in the garden bushes, but sat instead on the rooftop of a neighbor's house. Then I slept on a while with my eyes open.

143

And I thought to myself: there are no nightingales here, it's a blackbird.

But don't think this is the same story I already told you today! No—because just as I was thinking: there are no nightingales here, it's a blackbird—at that very moment, I woke up. It was four in the morning, daylight streamed into my eyes, sleep sank away as quickly as the last trace of a wave is soaked up by the dry sand at the beach. And there, veiled in daylight as in a soft woolen scarf, a blackbird sat in the open window! It sat there just as sure as I sit here now.

I am your blackbird—it said—don't you remember me?

I really didn't remember right away, but I felt happy all over while the bird spoke to me.

I sat on this window sill once before, don't you remember?—it continued, and then I answered: yes, one day you sat there just where you now sit, and I quickly closed the window, shutting it in.

I am your mother—it said.

This part, I admit, I may very well have dreamed. But the bird itself I didn't dream up; she sat there, flew into my room, and I quickly shut the window. I went up to the attic and looked for a large wooden bird cage that I seemed to remember, for the blackbird had visited me once before—in my childhood, like I just told you. She sat on my windowsill and then flew into my room, and I needed a cage. But she soon grew tame, and I didn't keep her locked up anymore, she lived free in my room and flew in and out. And one day she didn't come back again, and now she had returned. I had no desire to worry about whether it was the same blackbird; I found the cage and a new box of books to boot, and all I can tell you is that I had never before been such a good person as from that day on: the day I had my blackbird back again—but how can I explain to you what I mean by being a good person?

Did she often speak again?—Aone asked craftily.

No—said Atwo—she didn't speak. But I had to find birdfood for her and worms. You can imagine that it was

144

rather difficult for me: I mean the fact that she ate worms, and I was supposed to think of her as my mother—but it's possible to get used to anything, I tell you, it's just a matter of time—and don't most everyday matters likewise take getting used to! Since then I've never let her leave me, and that's about all I have to tell; this is the third story, and I don't know how it's going to end.

But aren't you implying—Aone cautiously inquired—that all this is supposed to have a common thread?

For God's sake, no—Atwo countered—this is just the way it happened; and if I knew the point of it all, then I wouldn't need to have told it in the first place. But it's like hearing a whisper and a rustling outside, without being able to distinguish between the two!